# YAMINO-KWITI

Sisítkano

FERNANDEÑO

SERRANO

Los Angeles. Yangna    Asuksa
Wenot    Siba                    Mukupiabet
Santa Monica    Akura    .Azusa    Kukomo    San Bernardino
                    Toibi    .Pomona
GABRIELINO                                        Wachbít

Redondo                                                        .Riverside
                        Hutuk    SANTA ANA RIVER                                        Banning .
Shua
San Pedro  Long Beach                Santa Ana                    TEMESCAL WASH

                                                LAKE
                                                ELSINORE
                                            Pieakhehe
PACIFIC            San Juan    SAN JUAN CREEK  JUANEÑO        LUISEÑO
                        Ahachmai                                        CAHUILLA

OCEAN                                                        Pala
                                    Wiawio    SAN LUIS REY RIVER
                                        Oceanside                        CUPEÑO

                        DIEGUEÑO

                                    SAN DIEGO RIVER
                                Nipawai
                                .San Diego

© 1983 Heyday Books

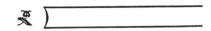

# YAMINO-KWITI
## A STORY OF INDIAN LIFE
## IN THE LOS ANGELES AREA

Written and illustrated

by

**Donna Preble**

HEYDAY BOOKS—BERKELEY,CALIFORNIA

ISBN: 0-930588-09-6
Library of Congress Catalog Card #83-080347
Printed in the United States of America

Heyday Books
Post Office Box 9145
Berkeley, California 94709


10 9 8 7 6 5 4 3 2 1

To the memory of my sister, ZAH-
RAH PREBLE HODGE, who loved the
Indians, and whose beautifully
compiled notes were my main
source of material. ¶ With a word
of gratitude to those dear friends
who made it possible for me to do
this work.

# Foreword

Since it was first published in 1940, *Yamino-Kwiti* has been widely praised as a true-to-life novel—true not only to the facts of Indian life in the Los Angeles area, but to the tone and spirit of that life as well. It reads easily—it is, after all, a fast-paced, suspenseful adventure story for older children. Yet when Alfred Kroeber, California's foremost anthropologist, wrote a foreword to the original edition of *Yamino-Kwiti*, he said of the "habits and manners" it presents:

> I cheerfully certify to their reliability. Before writing her story, the author absorbed the often recondite data with accuracy. Her hero is fictitious, but a Gabrielino boy of around 1760 would have lived, acted, seen, and participated in the life of his tribe as she describes Yamino-Kwiti doing. I know of no full-length piece of fiction concerned with the American Indian that is in better conformity with the ethnological facts.

*Yamino-Kwiti* is good fiction, good anthropology, and something more besides. It is wise. The wisdom may not be immediately apparent. Because *Yamino-Kwiti* is a novel, the author does not dazzle us with abstract insights or displays of scholarship. In fact one reads the book from cover to cover scarcely aware of the author at all. Yet gradually one comes to realize that behind the various characters and situations is someone who in the course of her life managed to attain deep understanding not just of the Gabrielino Indians, but indeed of human nature in general.

Donna Preble, the author and illustrator of *Yamino-Kwiti*, was born in 1882 in Reno, Nevada, and grew up in Berkeley, California. Her father was Surveyor-General of Nevada, prominent in the early history of the state; her mother was an artist, a painter of miniatures. "I was born with an unusual sense of color, form, and perspective," she wrote of herself. "I started drawing pictures as soon as I was given a slate and a pencil." She attended the Partington School of Illustration in San Francisco. In 1901, at the age of nineteen, she married, lived briefly in Hawaii where her husband taught at Oahu College, then returned to California. In 1916 they divorced, and she found herself alone with five children to support. She worked as a nurse, secretary, interior designer, and advertising illustrator and copywriter. She also went to night school where she studied writing. Life during these years was grueling. When later asked by *Who's Who* to list her most outstanding achievement, she replied: "There is none, unless one can count the raising and educating of five children alone."

It was the death of her sister, Zahrah Preble Hodge, in 1934 that led to *Yamino-Kwiti*. Zahrah was married to Frederick Webb Hodge, noted anthropologist and director of the Southwest Museum in Los Angeles. She had spent years collecting notes for what was intended to be a series of popular books about Indians of the West. Zahrah was to have done the writing, Donna the illustrating—and indeed they did collaborate on a book for very young children, *Tomar of Siba*. When Zahrah died, Donna took over the project completely, immersed herself in the notes, and out of them created *Yamino-Kwiti* "with a heart-ache that the work was not hers [Zahrah's], for she had so loved the thought of doing it." Yet it was in this book that the various strands of her own life came together; the scholarship of her sister, her early training as an illustrator, her skills as a writer, and most of all the experiences in her life that made her compassionate and at the same time realistic about human nature.

"I have learned that few people want to know the truth about anything," she once wrote in a letter, "but rather that they want their own prejudices and wishful thinking verified." She was a profound realist, but not a cynic. In the same letter she noted, "I love people and all the studies that relate to people." Her ability to love people without illusion is what makes *Yamino-Kwiti* so unusual. In order to appreciate the Native Californians, she did not have to romanticize them or idealize them. The characters in *Yamino-Kwiti* have real emotions, defects, and limitations; yet they are portrayed with dignity and affection. *Yamino-Kwiti* is one of those rare books that helps the reader appreciate Indian life for what it was, rather than for what many people would like it to have been. It still provides us with a thoroughly researched, vivid, and truthful picture of what Indian life in the Los Angeles area was like before the coming of whites.

Malcolm Margolin
Berkeley, California

# Contents

# Introduction

THIS STORY is about an Indian boy, Yamino - Kwiti, who lived in the valley of San Gabriel in southern California before the white men more than touched its shores. Yamino-Kwiti had heard the old men of his people tell of white men who came out of the western sea in great winged ships — "winged whales," the Indians called them. His grandfather's grandfather told the stories first.

The white men of these stories must have been Cabrillo, in 1542, and Vizcaíno, in 1602. Possibly some were Chinese voyagers in strange-looking junks that rose ghost-like out of the mists of the western horizon.

The early white explorers did not penetrate into the Indians' country, Cabrillo alone landing on Ballast Point at San Diego Harbor and on the islands off the coast farther north. The tales told of them, therefore, were like myths to the Indian children. They filled the listeners with awe of these unknown and not understood beings who sailed out of Nowhere over the rim of the world.

When the Spaniards finally penetrated inland, into the heart of the Indians' country, and came up from Baja California, with their civilized ways and different religion, the Indians did not know whether to greet them as enemies or friends. Their curiosity, however, was very great, and their desire to possess the baubles and gifts which the Spaniards offered brought them in contact with an influence which was to change the entire manner of Indian living and in time to bring an end to the Indian race.

It is interesting to think that at the time Yamino-Kwiti was playing and growing in his Indian way he had no knowledge of any world other than the uncultivated fields, the rough mountain slopes, and untraveled, arid deserts of the Western coast. Yet, on the Eastern coast of this same continent, a great nation was already started that would sweep westward in less than a century and dominate this unknown Indian country.

While Yamino-Kwiti was growing up, the English colonies were getting ready to fight England for their freedom. While the Indians of the West were living naked and free, the Indians of the East had long been familiar with the life and habits of the men who brought the Old World civilization to this country. These Eastern Indians were acquainted with the white man's satin coats, his lace collars and cuffs, his white powdered wigs, his houses built like palaces with metal tools and implements, his art and music, and his firearms.

Yamino-Kwiti and his playmates were as un-known to the people of the East as the Easterners were to the West, for there were great mountain ranges, wide plains, and swift rivers separating them.

Yamino-Kwiti was born in June, 1759. The In-dians did not count time as we do. Their years were unnumbered, stretching backward and for-ward into no one knew what, with no thought given to anything but the present. The months were reckoned by the moons, while the seasonal changes were marked by the sun. So it was that the month of Yamino-Kwiti's birth was not called June, but "Sintecar," meaning in the Gabrielino language, "the moon when the young eagles fly."

This Indian boy, Yamino-Kwiti, was just ten years old, as we reckon time, when the Spanish ex-plorer, Don Gaspar Portolá, and his great train of followers, came to the banks of the river now known as the Rio Hondo, which flowed past the village of Siba. Yamino-Kwiti saw white men, horses, and mules and heard a gun fired for the first time in his life.

# 1

## Yamino-Kwiti* Meets Hunar

YAMINO-KWITI was running just as fast as his nimble brown legs could take him. He had good reason to run, for he had just seen Hunar, the great grizzly.

Yamino-Kwiti had been eating honey. His small brown fingers were all sticky with it, and so was his face. When he had found the hollow tree with the little dark bees going in and out, he had jumped up and down with eagerness, for this was a feast dear to an Indian. He had taken the honeycomb out of the tree so carefully that not one of the little dark bees had been crushed. "If you do not hurt them," his father had told him, "they will not hurt you."

Then all of a sudden a terrible roar, like thunder, sounded right in his ear and made him jump. Hunar, the great bear, was almost at his shoulder, thrusting her huge nose toward the honey. Yamino-Kwiti did not know it was the honey she wanted. He was so frightened that he took to his heels as fast as he could go, almost tripping over one of Hunar's fat, roly-poly babies. Not stopping to see if Hunar were following him, he bounded down the

---

\* Yȧ-mee'-nȯ Quee'-tee.

trail, like an antelope. Sliding down the banks, and scratching his naked brown body, he splashed through the shallows of the river and ran into the village as though he could never stop.

"Hunar! Hunar!" he gasped.

"Hunar? Hunar?" The village folk took up his cry and passed it on. They crawled out of their huts or came running toward him from wherever they were. "Where? Where?" they cried.

They were all afraid of Hunar—so big, strong, and fierce an animal. There were many tales told about meeting Hunar on the mountain trails, and sometimes in the valley, as had Yamino-Kwiti. Sometimes those Indians who could not run as fast as Yamino-Kwiti never returned to the village— they had been crushed and clawed by Hunar. The Indian men did not hunt Hunar as they did Shukat, the deer. Usually Hunar stayed in the mountains —which the Indians called Xai and which the Spaniards later called the Sierra Madre—but if she had come to the honey tree, they said to one another, she was not very far away. "What shall we do?" they asked Siba-vik,[1] the chief, who stood in the center and listened to Yamino-Kwiti thoughtfully.

Amid much chatter and questioning, they finally turned to Pul Eraxbu, the wise old man of the village. He was so old that he knew all the secrets of the priesthood and many other things. He could

---

[1] See'-ba-veek. *See* Appendix for numerals.

tell them the stories of the world's creation, and who were the stars, the sun, and the moon. He could tell them how and when to hunt and how to make their weapons. He gave them charms to make their weapons strike true. And he told them now, "Have no fear. You see that Hunar did not follow Yamino-Kwiti. Hunar will not bring her babies to the village of men. Stay away from the honey tree, and Hunar will not touch you."

It was as he said. Just the same, Indian mothers gathered their Indian babies closer into the village and scolded them if they strayed from the sight of the elders. Grandmothers, sitting at the doors of their huts weaving baskets, watched

Grandmothers weaving baskets.

the little ones more closely than they did their basketmaking.

Indian youths got out their longest spears, tipped with sharp, obsidian points, and talked, wondering if their weapons were strong enough to kill Hunar. The young hunters bragged about what they could do, but the older ones said they had few weapons that could kill Hunar, whose hide was thick and head hard.

Tamít, the sun, went to bed, while Moar,* the moon, came out to shine on the round grass huts of the little village of Siba. Only the watcher at the fire remained out under the stars; all the others crawled through the low doorways of their huts to sleep inside, where they felt safer.

The night passed, with only Itaru, the coyote, howling his evening song in the wilderness. "Itaru talks to the Great Spirit," said the people in hushed voices as they huddled together in the darkness of their huts. The night passed, and the next, and the next, and Hunar did not come.

They all forgot about Hunar except Yamino-Kwiti, who did not forget. He dreamed about Hunar and how he had almost tripped over one of her babies, and he shivered in his sleep and drew his feet up quickly—so quickly that he woke himself, only to find that Wushi, his dog, was sleeping across his feet.

Nor did his mother forget Hunar. "It is well, Yamino-Kwiti," she said, "that you can run like the deer. You have the swift legs, like your father."

"Mother,"[2] he said to her, "do you think I shall be a courier like my father?"

---

* Mō'-àr.

"Perhaps," she answered, "if the Council of Elders and the chief do not choose you to go into the *Yobagnar*."[3]

"Oh, Mother, will they do that?"

"I do not know, Little Runner. You know it is the custom of our people to choose those boys who are strong and bright to teach them the secrets of the *Puplum*.[4] The *Puplum* grow old and die, and the young have to take their places."

Yamino-Kwiti looked thoughtful. He did not want to be a *Pul*,[4] to dance and sing at ceremonies; he wanted to be a courier like his father. He wanted to see all the country outside his village about which his father had told him such wonderful stories. He thought of the porpoises that circled

The porpoise that swam round the world.

around the edge of the world to watch over it and see that all was well. If he could just go to the very edge of the world in one of those big plank canoes that the shore people built and see the porpoises! Ah, that would be much better than being a *Pul!* He sighed and hoped he would not be selected for the *Puplum*. Most of the old men in the *Puplum* were cross.

"Put down your ear, close," he said to his mother. With one hand he pushed her glossy black hair away from her ear and whispered, "Think you that Hunar could be old Pul Tauwaro? When Pul Tauwaro was alive he used to growl at me and the other boys, just like Hunar. What think you, Mother?"

She laughed merrily and then clapped her hand over her mouth lest someone hear and ask what was so funny. "Sh-sh, Yamino-Kwiti. It might be," she whispered to him. "I do not know. It is what our people say they do. That is why we do not eat bear meat."

"Yes, I know," he said. "Just the same, Hunar growled like old Pul Tauwaro." Privately he hoped with all his heart that the hunters would find Hunar and have such a fight that they would have to kill the bear. But he knew, even while he wished it, that they would not kill Hunar if they could help it.

As the days passed, nearly everyone in the village forgot Hunar and went about his business. The children played, or hunted insects, grasshoppers, lizards, snakes, and other things that were easy to catch and good to eat.

Pul Eraxbu, who talked to the moon, told the chief to send Ya'iikat, the crier, out from the *Yobagnar* to tell the women it was time to gather food in the fields, and that the men should get ready to hunt. At sunset Yamino-Kwiti could hear the crier going from hut to hut calling out, loud and strong in his harsh voice, for all to worship in the *Yobagnar* early in the morning. He swung his *mom-lah-pish*,⁵ or bull- roarer, around and around, making a great noise and waking up the Indian babies in their willow baskets.

That night, while the whole village slept, Wushi stirred and growled. This woke Yamino-Kwiti, who sat up in the dark and listened. Was there some animal outside the hut? Yamino-Kwiti thought of Hunar, the bear; of Tukut, the panther —the two animals the Indians most dreaded. Yet, in spite of his acute hearing, he heard no sound except the soft rustling of leaves in the breeze. But Wushi stood at the door of the hut with bristling back.

Quietly Yamino-Kwiti threw aside his rabbit-skin blanket and on hands and knees crept through the low door to the heels of Wushi. "I mustn't wake Father and Mother," he thought to himself. With his hand on Wushi's cold nose and with a motion for him to be silent, Yamino-Kwiti listened. Except for the stars, the night was still and dark. The oak trees threw a dense blackness under their branches.

"Hoo-hoo-hoo oo-oo," said a soft, mournful voice, and Yamino-Kwiti looked up to see Muhut, the big owl, silently flap his wings and take off from the big oak, flitting somewhere between his hut and that of *Ni-apa*,² "my older brother," so-called by Yamino-Kwiti's father, but whom the rest of the tribe called Koti-Cuit.*

"Hoo-hoo-hoo oo-oo," came again from somewhere off in the dark. It was the most mournful, foreboding sound a bird could make. The Indians did not regard the owl as they did other birds—to be caught for food; it was an eerie, ghostly thing of the night, and when it spoke its sad and sorrowful notes over a hut, it was a sign that someone from that hut would meet death before long.

Yamino-Kwiti could not be sure which dwelling the big bird had marked for its sad prophecy, so he squatted in the dark and wondered.

"Hoo-hoo-hoo oo-oo," he heard again. Its dark shadow flitted between him and the stars overhead, alighting on the very top of the grass hut of Koti-Cuit. Yamino-Kwiti's heart beat fast, for he was fond of his uncle—and his uncle's son, Puku-Kakar, was his cousin and playmate.

"O Koti-Cuit," said Yamino-Kwiti to himself, "I like you."[6] He thought, too, of the others in that hut—the wife, the children, the old mother and father of Koti-Cuit, who were also his own grandfather and grandmother. He had affection for them all and did not wish to think that Muhut, the owl, had selected any one of them for Tucupar, the Indian heaven.

"I shall not tell anyone," he said to himself as he crawled back into his hut. Wushi, however,

---

* Kō'-tee-Kweet.

Nearly everyone in the village forgot Hunar and went about his
business.

He saw one of them stoop at the fire.

still growled and would not follow. "There *is* someone there," thought Yamino-Kwiti and renewed his hold on the nose of Wushi. He crouched at the door listening and waiting.

Evidently no one had heard the owl but himself, for the entire village was silent. Even the watcher at the fire was sleeping quietly with his chin buried in his breast, squatting like a carved idol before the low-burning fire.

A faint rustle of leaves under the oak made Wushi prick up his ears and raise the hair on his back.

"Be still!" Yamino-Kwiti urged him, making himself as much a part of the shadows as possible.

Then Yamino-Kwiti saw a strange thing. Two dark figures, only a little darker than the shadows around them, crept from under the spreading branches of the oak and stepped toward the sleeping watcher of the fire. Yamino-Kwiti had to keep a firm hand on Wushi to hold him. Yamino-Kwiti was only a boy—how did he know but that these shadowy figures were some of the *Puplum* at their magic, and that to interfere would be dangerous? He saw one of the figures stoop at the fire and linger for a brief moment. A small blaze flared up, and the figure darted away with a burning brand in his hand, running toward the hut of Koti-Cuit. Still Yamino-Kwiti crouched and wondered. Was it Pul Maat?* What was he doing?

* Pool Mah'-at.

He saw a sudden glare of light, and the two figures darting away into the night from the blaze they had started. He saw the light of the fire reflected an instant on their bare backs as they fled. Then Yamino-Kwiti let Wushi loose with a yell.

"Catch them, Ni-Wushi, catch them!" he yelled, and, reaching for his bow and arrows, he called, "My father! Go to Koti-Cuit!"

His cry and Wushi's loud yapping woke the village. Barking dogs and excited men and women came crawling out of their houses to see the blazing hut of Koti-Cuit which lighted the entire area of the village. Koti-Cuit was dragging out his people and their possessions as fast as it was possible, for the fire was quick and hot.

In the meantime Yamino-Kwiti took after Wushi and the two dim figures. So dark was the night he could not have followed them had it not been for Wushi's noise and the glare of the fire behind him. He saw them suddenly outlined against the white blossoms of the sage. Quickly Yamino-Kwiti drew bow and fitted an arrow. Ping!

A sharp cry and the smaller of the two figures dropped out of sight in the tall grass. While Yamino-Kwiti came up to the fallen form, Wushi was wrangling over the other. Yamino-Kwiti had a hard time pulling the dog from his prey.

"Yamino-Kwiti! Where are you?" came his father's voice.

"Here!" he answered. "Come quickly, come quickly!"

Then came the others, carrying torches, and excitedly asking questions. The smaller of the two figures got quickly to his feet, and, before anyone could stop him, he disappeared into the dark shadows of the trees by the river, while a shower of arrows followed him. The larger one was carried to the village and bound hand and foot to await the daylight.

Koti-Cuit's hut was burned to the ground. His wife and his two children had come out without injury, but the two old people had been badly burned in their effort to rescue their treasured possessions. They were turned over to A-nub-su-voi-rot, the medicine man, who took them to his hut to tend to their injuries in his own peculiar manner.

Koti-Cuit and his family were given shelter in the hut of the courier, Mamish-Ahikañ.[7] Yamino-Kwiti found his cousin, Puku-Kakar, sharing his mat and rabbitskin blanket. But there was little sleep for anyone the rest of the night, for even the grownups were excited and full of questions as to why the fire had occurred.

"It was the family's enemy from Asuksa,"[8] said the courier to his brother, Koti-Cuit. "They wanted to wipe out our father and our mother and you. They will try something on me, next."

"We shall have a song fight,"[9] said Koti-Cuit.

"That will cause them to feel the displeasure of our god, and they will die from sheer unworthiness."

"What will you do with the prisoner?" asked Puku-Kakar.

"He is well bound," said Koti-Cuit. "He cannot get away, and when we return from our hunting, Siba-vik will hold council and dispose of him."

"Now all go to sleep," said Mamish-Ahikañ, for there is the hunting in the morning—not even our enemies can keep us from success at our hunting."

Hunter with a deer.

# 2

## Up a Tree

THE FOLLOWING morning the men came out of their huts armed with bows and arrows, while their bodies were well painted with white and blue horizontal stripes. They looked like strange demons and would have scared a white person into hysterics, but even the Indian babies were used to them, and all the village thought them wonderful!

The hunters ate no food, nor would they touch a mouthful until they returned from the hunt. Led by their chief, Siba-vik, they fell into line, running one behind the other. Yamino-Kwiti, Tomear,[10] Puy-Puy, and all the other children followed along behind the last one, but when they reached the *Yoba*, they had to stop. The children were not allowed to go near the entrance of the sacred place, except those few who were being trained for the sacred dances and songs. Should they disobey and approach too near, they were punished.

Yamino-Kwiti wanted very much to see what the men did before they went to hunt, but he knew better than to stay near enough to listen. He thought of climbing a tree and watching from there, but that would be a worse crime than the

other. So he stayed where he was, his bare toes
digging into the dirt in his eagerness, while the
rest of his body was as still as the little rabbit's
when he is listening with his ears pricked up.

His mother saw Yamino-Kwiti and, knowing
his great curiosity, called to him: "Yamino-Kwiti!
Use those legs of yours and get away from there,
quickly!" He and the rest of the children drew
back fearfully.

He scowled, for he was just a bit defiant and
resentful. If they were going to choose him to go
into the *Yobagnar* he wanted to know beforehand
what it was all about. He knew it was a great
honor to be chosen, yet he was sure he would not
like the *Yobagnar*. What went on in there sounded
mysterious and awful.

Had he been able to take a peek through the
willow poles that formed the fence of the *Yoba*
around the *Yobagnar*, he would have seen strange
antics, indeed. Pul Eraxbu had drawn a crude
figure in sand on the ground before the rough
wooden image of Kwawar,[11] the Great Spirit.

When the men came prancing into the *Yoba*
they ran around the enclosure until they were opposite the image and the figure drawn upon the
ground. The chief then gave a jump and, spring-
ing high into the air, shouted loudly and waved
his weapons. Landing nimbly on his feet he drew
his bow and pointed his arrow upward. Each
hunter in the procession followed the leader until

the whole enclosure held what looked like painted
Indian statues in the position of shooting their
arrows at the sky.

When the men had finished their ceremony, the
women came. Yamino-Kwiti, with childish per-
sistency, walked with his mother, but she sent him
away, and the other women frowned at him. He
stood, then, with the other children under a big
oak tree and watched the women form in line behind their leader. They did much as the men did,
but did not run or jump. Instead, they went slowly, with regular, dignified steps. The children
stood on both sides of the line and watched, their
black eyes wide and solemn with interest. They
watched until the women disappeared through the
opening in the *Yoba* fence, and then, because the
*Yoba* seemed quiet, they scattered and ran here
and there about the village, leaving only Yamino-
Kwiti standing under the tree, wondering.

Inside the *Yoba* the women presented Kwawar
with their sticks and wands. That the idol neither
moved nor spoke his thanks from wooden lips did
not lessen the faith of his worshipers. He was but
an image of Kwawar, whom they could not see.
Their part now done, they all scattered and went
their ways, sure in their hearts and minds that
their efforts at gathering food would be successful.

The women went to the fields, some with babies
in baskets on their backs. As it was the Moon of
Showers, or April,[12] they went where the wild let-

The women went to the fields with babies
on their backs.

tuce and water cress grew lush in the shallows by
the river. They gathered the wild clover in the
fields, blossoms and all, dug up the onionlike roots
of the swaying blue brodiaea, and picked the young
plants of both the golden poppy and the heavenly
blue lupine so that their families might have fresh
green food. And the children helped the women,
but Yamino-Kwiti was not among them.

Before the women had emerged from the *Yoba*
he had grown tired waiting, and, hearing the men
laughing in their preparations for departure, he
had run to watch them. They had gathered together the false deer heads[13] they used in their
hunting, and all their bows and arrows and long
spears. Now they were stinging themselves with
nettles all over their painted bodies in order to
make them more keen and watchful at their hunting, even stinging the lids of their eyes that they
might see better and more quickly. So long had
this been a custom it did not occur to any of them
to doubt the results.

They laughed loudly to cover up the pain and
discomfort they felt and bragged rashly about the
deer, antelope, rabbits, and quail they would bring
back from the hunt. Some of the men were brave
of heart and hoped, privately, they would see
Hunar and perhaps have to kill the great bear in
a good fight. Her coat of grizzly fur would make
a warm mat to lie on or become a valuable article
for trade with the island people from Pimu.[14]

Some of them were not so brave and were afraid they would see Hunar, but they said nothing and hid their fear with much bragging and loud laughter, for no Indian would let another know that he ever feared anything. They merely said it was not wise to kill Hunar, even if they should meet the animal, lest they hurt a human being who had died and had come back to live in the great body of Hunar. They were glad to believe this, for it covered up their terror of the huge creature, who could stand on hind legs and walk like a giant. However, it was not likely that they would see Hunar, for in the Green Grass Moon[11] the little bear cubs are not yet two moons old, and Hunar keeps them out of sight of man and beast.

Yamino-Kwiti determined to follow the men and ran to his father's hut to get his throwing stick.[15] With all the cunning of a grown Indian, he followed by gliding unseen from bush to bush and from tree to tree. There was an open space between him and the last Indian. He measured it with his eye, saw the back of the last Indian disappear in the chaparral, and made a dash for cover behind a big toyon-berry bush on the edge of the trail. Bang! He felt the sudden impact of another body against his own and with a bumped head went sprawling full length on the ground. Hastily pulling himself into a sitting position, he looked to see what had hit him.

There sat Puku-Kakar opposite him, rubbing

his head and looking as surprised as Yamino-Kwiti. Each boy had been heading for the same bush for cover. They laughed aloud, then clapped their hands over their mouths lest they be heard.

"Puku - Kakar!" exclaimed Yamino - Kwiti. "Were you following the hunters, too?"

Before he could answer, there stood Pul Maat before them. He said not a word, but folded his arms across his chest and looked first at one boy, then the other.

They got to their feet. There was no need for any words. They knew that their venture was over. They picked up their throwing sticks and started back along the trail. When Yamino-Kwiti looked back, Pul Maat was still standing as they had left him, arms folded and a scowl on his face.

It was not until they lost sight of him that the boys spoke to one another. "Ugh!" said Yamino-Kwiti. "It would be Pul Maat who'd spoil our fun!"

"What shall we do now?" asked Puku-Kakar.

"We'll cross the river," said Yamino-Kwiti, who was always ready with an idea, "and go up the hill. One time my father and I were there, and we saw the honeybees swarming around a hollow tree. We shall find some honey."

"Yum-m-m," said Puku - Kakar, patting his stomach. "Come on!"

They knew that they should return to the village and help with the food gathering in the fields,

but the day was bright and cool and filled them
with a desire for adventure.

The hunters had gone north from the village,
and the women had spread out in the fields to the
northwest, so Yamino-Kwiti and Puku-Kakar
went south, skirting east of the village, until they
came to the river.[16] They waded through the shallow water of the wash, carefully avoiding the
profusion of round stones under their feet. When
they came to the deeper channel they swam and
played in the stream, enjoying the feel of the cool
water on their bare bodies.

Tamít, the sun, was climbing high in his bright
blue trail, so the boys took their throwing sticks
and left the wash behind them, finding their way
through the thick grass and the reeds and scaring
the wild fowl from their swampy retreats. On
they went, boisterously finding their way through
the willows and cottonwood trees that lined the
little creek at the foot of the hill.[17]

Yamino-Kwiti was sure he knew where to find
the honey tree that he and his father had seen,
but the thickness of the underbrush and trees on
this northern slope of the hills confused him. The
only path they found was one used, evidently, by
wild animals when they went down the hill to the
creek for water.

Both boys knew it was against all Indian custom for two small boys to wander so far away
alone, but they sought to forget that by thinking

and talking of the honey they would bring back to the village.

In some places the little crooked path was like a leafy tunnel through the brush. It led them out, finally, into a small, open space where the sun shone warmly on the grass. Suddenly Puku-Kakar grasped Yamino-Kwiti by the arm.

"Look!" he whispered, pointing to the grass at their feet which was flattened and mussed, showing an imprint where a body had lain. The two boys stood silent and quiet, wondering. Suddenly the faint, unmistakable twang of a bowstring sounded. Instantly the boys dropped flat on the ground, and an arrow struck quivering in the trunk of the tree behind them, barely missing them. They did not dare move! They were sure they were still in their own territory, and no member of their own tribe would so wantonly shoot another!

On the grass where the unknown person had lain was a gourd partly filled with water, a fiber-woven packet such as some of the men wore fastened to a belt, and a pipe.

The two boys looked at each other, their faces close to the green grass. "We must get away from here," whispered Yamino-Kwiti, barely doing more than move his lips. "He'll be coming back!"

Cautiously, silently, they slid backwards on their stomachs until they were again in the little path among the underbrush. Now they dared

stand up. Beside them was the trunk of a sycamore tree. Birds were twittering in the branches
overhead. Just above them a ruby-throated hum-
mingbird poised on invisible wings. Their eyes
followed it as it flew upward, and then Yamino-
Kwiti had an inspiration which he acted upon
immediately.

He began to climb the sycamore and motioned
to his cousin to follow him. Quietly they climbed,
and, except for the sudden stilling of the birds,
one would never have known that the large green
leaves of the sycamore hid two small Indians.
When they had climbed as high as they could and
still be hidden among the leaves, they peered cautiously through the leafy curtain at the grassy
spot they had just left.

Two Indians entered the open space. Yamino-
Kwiti recognized one of them as a man from
Asuksa, but the other was a stranger to him. They
immediately examined the unmistakable marks
the boys had left behind them. Suddenly one of
them laughed. With a hand covered with shell
and bone rings he pointed to the print of a small
hand and said, *"Nio mare!*[18] Just babies!"

The effect of that speech on the two boys was
immediate. Yamino-Kwiti opened his mouth with
indrawn breath and closed it suddenly into a grim
straight line, the picture of insulted dignity. Puku-
Kakar scowled, thrust his chin forward and,
noiselessly moving his lips, repeated: "Babies!"

The boys glared at each other. They would show the men they were not babies! But how? They were up in the tree unable to move, or come down, as long as the two strangers were within earshot.

A hard test of their endurance was before them. The two strange Indians proceeded to make themselves comfortable in the small open space. They were eating something. The boys peered hungrily through the leaves of the sycamore. Honey! The strangers had found the honey tree! And the sounds they made told plainly their enjoyment of it.

This was almost too much for the boys in the tree. What with their growing discomfort at having to stay in one position, not daring to move, the sight of the feast of honey made their mouths water. What could they do? They dared not come down; they could do nothing but wait. Finding the tree quiet and still, the birds came back and twittered and hopped about the children who clung so silently in the tree.

Tamít, the sun, passed slowly, so slowly, overhead and began his descent toward the west, and still the Indians stayed on. The boys had overheard a conversation, however, which had left them excited and had helped them to endure the tedium of waiting. They dared not speak, but the interchange of their glances was eloquent.

"We shall wait till it is dark," said the stranger who wore so many ornaments on his hands and arms.

"But now there are few people in the village,"
said the other. "I watched and saw the men go
on their hunt and the women to the fields! It is a
good time now—so few there!"

"Yes, but they have left a guard," said the first,
"and all the old people. They can shoot arrows as
well as the hunters, and they could see us a long
way in the daytime! No, we shall wait until it
is dark."

So they waited, and the boys waited.

One of the strangers stretched out in the warm
sunshine and went to sleep, but the other sat and
wound some sinew about a feathered arrow shaft.
Wouldn't he ever get tired? The boys almost fell
asleep themselves.

They were nearly ready to cry with fatigue
when the man put aside his arrow shaft and lay
down. He raised his arms over his head, stretched,
yawned, and lay for a while looking at the sky.
On that warm, sunny day such a position was
sure to put anyone to sleep, and it was only a
moment or two before the man was entirely relaxed, breathing heavily and regularly. He was
sound asleep. Then the boys started to climb
quietly down the tree, but stopped suddenly—the
tree was shaking!

Looking down through the leaves and branches
they could see an immense, furry black back rubbing against the trunk of the sycamore. The tree
shivered furiously, but the boys clung tightly and

made no sound, and the shaking soon ceased, for the huge creature below was only scratching its back.

Peering through their leafy screen, they saw two tiny roly-poly bear cubs emerge into the open space where the two men slept peacefully. The cubs had smelled the honey, and now the largest one gamboled up to the nearest Indian as he lay sprawled on the grass and began to lick the honey still smeared on his face.

He awoke with a start, saw the little bear face close to his own, while behind it, rearing up hugely like a giant above him, ready to charge, was Hunar! With a cry of fright the man sprang up and dived into the brush. The other Indian, awakened by his companion's cry, fled also, a close second behind. He was barely in time to miss the lightninglike quickness of Hunar's charge, but as the men disappeared in the brush, Hunar turned to protect her cubs, which she seldom left for a moment.

The two boys in the tree suppressed their boyish giggles lest Hunar hear them. Yamino-Kwiti had not forgotten the time Hunar had frightened him in much the same way. They knew that small bears could climb trees, but would Hunar try to climb the sycamore? Hunar, however, was on guard for her cubs, while they nosed the grassy spot and licked up all the honey they could find. The boys had another long wait.

They hoped with all their hearts that, when Hunar did decide to leave, she would not take the path under their tree, for it was along this path they must travel to get back to the village. It was imperative now that they return before the hunters, for they had a warning to give. It was, however, after sunset and beginning to get dark before Hunar finally took her cubs and ambled through the brush.

The boys lost no time in scrambling down the tree and getting back to Siba.

Bear with cubs.

With bumped heads they went sprawling on the ground.

Someone touched his arm.

# 3

# The Prisoner Escapes

I N THE VILLAGE the children and the women were busily occupied, having returned with full baskets from the fields. The babies in their willow cradles had blinked at the sun all day and were now either asleep or rubbing their little brown noses with still browner little fists.

The women were preparing for the return of the hunters. They had brought a goodly supply of wood for the fires, which were already burning. Stone bowls stood close against the coals, and waterproof baskets stood with water in them awaiting the moment when the hot stones, buried among the coals of the fire, should be dropped into the water to make it boil. The women were bustling about, tending to fires, children, babies, and all the necessary duties of the Indian women. The growing darkness added to the confusion.

It was in the midst of this activity that the two boys slipped into the village unnoticed. Tired as they were, they were bursting with importance, for the warning must be given quickly—perhaps it was already too late. But no—the prisoner was still tied securely to the tree.

Yamino-Kwiti, with Puku-Kakar close at his elbow, looked for his father, but the men had not returned. Then he sought his mother and found her, busy and inattentive, among the stone pots and the firewood.

"Mother," said Yamino-Kwiti.

"Run away, Yamino-Kwiti," she said. "Don't bother——" Then she stopped and looked at him. "Where have you been all day? You were not in the fields."

"We went to get some honey——" But he was not to be allowed to finish, nor to tell his story, for just then a great shout went up. "The men! Here they come!"

Immediately turmoil and confusion began, and Yamino-Kwiti's mother paid no more attention to him, but shouted, sang, and danced with the others, for were not the hunters returning?

The two boys looked at each other with disgust and despair. Each time they tried to tell their tale to someone they were pushed aside, and finally Pul Maat scolded them for getting in the way. "Go back where you belong," he said in his cross voice. "You must not get in the way of the elders!" And before the boys could tell their news he had waved them away and turned on his heel to join the others around the fire.

There was nothing for the boys to do but obey. They had twice incurred the displeasure of Pul Maat this day, so they stood in the outer shadows and watched in silence the activity about the fire —two very hungry boys.

The hunters were careful not to skin and prepare their own game lest they accidentally eat that which they themselves had killed. Each selected something of another's, and then began the skinning and preparing of food for the hungry and tired men.

During this excitement the prisoner was forgotten. All day he had been taunted and tortured by the old men, women, and children. He had been securely tied to the trunk of a tree. His wounds which had been inflicted by the sharp teeth of Wushi must have been hard for him to endure, but not a sign did he make of suffering.

The hungry hunters waited impatiently about the fires. Not one of them could have been more hungry than the prisoner, whose eyes were fixed on the treetops lest the sight of food torture him more. He swallowed now and then as the fragrance of wood smoke, rabbit stew, and sizzling deer meat wafted about the hamlet, and his nostrils quivered, but not a sound did he make.

The darkness of the night settled about the village, but men, women, and children were still eating, laughing, singing, and even getting up now and then to dance about the fires. The tired body of the prisoner slumped forward no longer able to keep awake, now that there was no one to taunt him. Suddenly he started, all his senses alert!

Someone had touched his arm with a whispered "Sh-sh!"

He saw a hand ornamented with many shell and bone rings come from behind him and loosen the cords that bound him so tightly. They fell at his feet. Softly, with eyes now alert, watching the group about the fire where even the dogs were busy gnawing bones and growling over them, the prisoner slipped silently as a shadow behind the tree and into the darkness beyond the circle of the firelight. He followed another silent shadow,

Stone bowls by the fire.

and the two were soon lost among the dark trees along the riverbank.

When his absence was finally discovered it was too late and too dark to track him. Yamino-Kwiti and Puku-Kakar had long been sleeping, curled up close together like two little cubs. They had fallen asleep on the ground while watching the feast.

# 4

# The Council

**T**HE NEXT DAY when most of the hunters were lazily drowsing in the warm sunshine, which they loved to do, Siba-vik called a council. A runner was sent to Asuksa to request the presence of their chief, Asuksa-vik.

Yamino-Kwiti was also summoned and questioned as to what he had seen at the time of the burning of his uncle's hut. He felt very important, stood very straight, and told his story simply. Siba-vik observed him with favor, and Pul Maat gloated in his heart as he watched the slim little figure with bright eyes and heard the quick, straightforward answers. "He'll do well in the *Yobagnar*," he thought to himself. "We'll make a *Pul* of him."

When Asuksa-vik came the two chiefs held a conference. Yamino-Kwiti was again questioned, this time by Asuksa-vik. He did not feel so important when Asuksa-vik finished questioning him, for that stocky, thickset chief refused to accept the testimony of a mere child. Yamino-Kwiti drew himself up and glared at Asuksa-vik.

The *Puplum* were drawn into the conference for advice. They talked among themselves in a language only they could understand, but neither the *Puplum* nor the two chiefs could come to any agreement regarding the incident, or to a settlement. Had the culprits been tribal enemies they would have been tortured and shot with arrows, but being of the same tribe and members of a family feud only, the punishment was a matter to be decided.

According to custom, it became necessary to call in a third chief from a distant hamlet. A runner was sent hurrying to Akura[8] to fetch their chief, Akura-vik. The two chiefs and the council resigned themselves to accepting the decision, whatever it might be, of the third chief.

It was late in the afternoon before Akura-vik[1] arrived. He swaggered a bit, for he felt the importance of being the deciding factor in a quarrel between two chiefs as important as Siba-vik and Asuksa-vik. He was not so stocky as Asuksa-vik. He came heavily laden with strings of beads and shells around his neck and eagle feathers in his headdress.

He seated himself before the two chiefs, the *Puplum* and the council forming a circle about them all. Siba-vik stated the testimony of Yamino-Kwiti; Asuksa-vik refused to accept it. Akura-vik listened and then finally lifted his hand in a gesture for silence. "Where is the boy?" he asked.

Again Yamino-Kwiti came forward. He had never seen Akura-vik before and was fascinated by the little shell beads strung in long strings about his neck and by the strange, deep scars on his arms, one of which was shaped like an eagle. But he looked the imposing man in the eye and stood as straight as his father's long arrows.

"Did anyone else beside yourself see who started the fire?" he asked Yamino-Kwiti.

"Ni-Wushi, my dog, saw them," said Yamino-Kwiti.

Akura-vik turned to Siba-vik. "Had you no watcher at the fire?" he asked.

They had all forgotten the watcher at the fire! Now he was summoned and came sleepily from his hut, for he slept in the daytime that he might keep awake at night.

He refused to admit that he had slept, saying that he had no idea how the fire started. Yamino-Kwiti was too astounded to say a word for a moment, but opened his eyes wide in surprise. He knew better than to call an older person *yayare*, meaning "one who did not tell the truth," so he said nothing.

Akura-vik looked at Yamino-Kwiti. "Did you see this watcher, also?" he asked. Yamino-Kwiti nodded silently with his eyes on the face of the watcher. "Yes, I saw him."

"What was he doing?" asked Akura-vik.

Yamino-Kwiti squatted on his heels and let his

head droop on his breast in the same manner as that of the watcher at the fire. He closed his eyes. There was a little rumble of laughter among the council. But Yamino-Kwiti was as solemn as a little owl.

"You may go," said Akura-vik.

"Yes, you may go," repeated Siba-vik, and Yamino-Kwiti jumped up and left the circle, glad to be free, for he had been questioned and been made to repeat his story so often he wanted to find Puku-Kakar and the other boys and run and shout.

In the end Akura-vik decided to accept the testimony of Yamino-Kwiti. The two brothers who had burned the hut had shown unmistakable evidence of having been wounded, and they could neither give a straight account of what they had done, nor where they had been the night of the fire.

"You will have the culprits pay Koti-Cuit for his house," he told Asuksa-vik. "They will divide the payment between them, and it will be as much as the goods which were destroyed were worth. You will punish the watcher at the fire as you see fit."

Koti-Cuit then was asked to give an account of

Money beads.

what was destroyed. He listed deerskins, baskets, bows and arrows, seeds and meal, and many other articles which, though of smaller value, would take some time to replace. The payment was to be four *ponko*,[19] or a *sayako*—each *ponko*, or string of money beads, as long as the arm of Koti-Cuit— and this decision had to be accepted, for such was their government.

# 5

# Indian Stories

**E**ARLY one morning Yamino-Kwiti crawled out of his father's hut. Jumping nimbly to his feet, he looked toward the purple-blue mountains where the first flush of dawn tinged the clouds with rosy hues. There was a great twittering of birds among the trees. The morning breeze blew fresh across the valley, rustled the stiff dark leaves of the oaks, and fluttered the silver-lined leaves of the cottonwoods until they seemed to shiver in the cool of the morning.

A brave but foolish little rabbit hopped daringly near the Indian wickiups. There he is, that little cottontail! See him standing on his haunches with his forepaws like little hands lifted in prayer? Quick, or he'll be gone!

Yamino-Kwiti cautiously picked up his throwing stick. Carefully, silently taking aim, he poised his small, lithe body ready to throw the stick. There it goes! Yam! The little rabbit gave just one, small, surprised bound and crumpled silently among the wild flowers to be caught up instantly by eager hands.

"Mother!" Yamino-Kwiti called, "I killed a rabbit for breakfast!"

"What a good hunter you are getting to be, Yamino-Kwiti," said his mother, crawling out of the hut on her hands and knees. "Like your father, you are." There was pride in her voice, for all the village called the swift-footed father of Yamino-Kwiti, Mamish-Ahikañ, who was as swift with his arrows as he was with his feet.

"Come," she said as she rose to her feet. "We shall skin him quickly, for that makes another skin for our blanket and a good breakfast for your father."

"Mother, only once did I throw!" He held the rabbit up by its long ears so that the little paws hung down limp. Yamino-Kwiti touched them with his finger and ran his hand over the soft fur of the rabbit's back. One more skin, soft and warm, to add to the pile, and a good rabbit stew to warm his insides. He had started the morning well.

He had not seen old Pul Maat standing in the shadows of the near-by oak, nor did he see him leave as silently as he came. But Father Mockingbird knew he had gone and so had flown into the nesting place to talk it over with Mother Mockingbird.

Yamino-Kwiti heard their chatter. "Listen, Mother, the mockingbird says, 'Pul-Maat, Pul-Maat, Pul-Maat.' Hear him?"

His mother laughed. "To me he says, 'Come-and-eat, come-and-eat, come-and-eat,' and now—listen! He's saying, 'Take-your-bath, take-your-bath, take-your-bath.' "

But only Father Mockingbird knew which of them was correct.

Later in the morning the father of Yamino-Kwiti met Pul Maat on the trail leading under the shade of the willows by the riverbank.

"That boy of yours," said Pul Maat. "I have watched him. He throws his throwing stick quickly and true. He is equally sure with his arrows. Perhaps we shall choose him. . . . We shall watch him a little longer."

They parted in the usual Indian manner. "*Yamu uimi*,[20] I go," said Pul Maat. "*Mea*, go!" answered the courier and went down the trail. Pul Maat turned and watched him go.

The courier was very thoughtful when he looked at his son that evening. It was a great honor the *Puplum* were conferring upon his son. If they were to choose Yamino-Kwiti for official duties in the *Yobagnar* he must begin to teach him some of the things he would need to know. So far he had only told him of his own adventures as he ran long distances on errands for his chief, carrying messages by word of mouth to other chiefs in the far villages. He must begin to tell him of the legends of the tribe. He could hear the boys shouting at their play out in the clearing.

"Children," he called, "come and hear some stories."

"Come on!" yelled Tomear to Puku-Kakar.

"Come on!" called Puku-Kakar to Puy-Puy, who motioned with his arm to the others to come.

The Indian children were no different from other children all over the world who love to hear stories. It did not take them long to gather in a noisy group about the fire in front of the courier's hut.

The mother of Yamino-Kwiti put more wood on the fire. As the children gathered about it she managed to whisper to Yamino-Kwiti, "Listen, listen well, my son, for you are to remember each word."

Ordinarily the Indian children were not allowed the warmth of the fire lest they rob some of it from their elders, or lest they make themselves less rugged, but tonight was a storytelling night, and the light and warmth of the fire were for them and the storyteller only.

In the distance could be heard the chilling cry of Itaru,* the coyote—a hysterical chorus from one lone throat.

"Listen to Itaru," said Yamino-Kwiti.

"Know you why Itaru howls?" asked the courier.

No one spoke. His father looked at Yamino-Kwiti. "I think, Father," said Yamino-Kwiti, "that he is laughing at us." And the eerie cry did

---

* I-tar'-oo.

sound like wild, mocking laughter. The storyteller nodded.

"Listen, and I shall tell you about Itaru. No one knows what he says, except the wise old men of the *Puplum*, but he goes out alone in the night to talk to . . ." his voice sank to a whisper, and little thrills went up and down the bare, brown backs of the Indian children, ". . . to talk to Y-yo-ha-rivg-nain."

The real Indian word for God was *Kwawar*,[11] but this sacred name was never spoken aloud. Instead, they said in hushed voices, "Y-yo-ha-rivg-nain," which means "the Giver of Life."

In the soft, hushed silence that followed the mention of the sacred name, the children looked at one another and back again to the speaker. Their bright black eyes, wide with interest, shone in the firelight. They drew closer together, but no word nor sound was made by any of them, now that the storytelling had begun. They could all hear Itaru far off in the moonlight on some rising mesa fragrant with sage and wild lilac, singing to Y-yo-ha-rivg-nain his evening lament, like the cry of lost babies.

The courier paused a moment while Yamino-Kwiti's mother put more wood on the fire, but no one noticed her, for they were looking at the story-teller who, although he glanced at each child in turn, seemed to be telling the story straight to Yamino-Kwiti.

"One time," said the courier, "a friend of Itaru told him a story of his adventures. He had traveled far, this friend, and had seen a tribe of tall, handsome people who derived their greatness from a ball of fire that gave them warmth and light.

"Itaru listened to this tale and determined to obtain that wonderful ball for himself. Very cunningly he learned the whereabouts of this tribe and made a journey to the place. He slyly changed his shape, entered their abode and, grabbing the ball in his teeth, ran swiftly away.

"This act of Itaru," the courier went on, "caused a great war among the Indian peoples. The wronged tribe made so much trouble for all the others by trying to get back their fire ball that Itaru found himself in great difficulties. He did not know where to hide it to keep it safely. So he sought the guidance of the Giver of Life, Y-yo-ha-rivg-nain.

"Climbing to the top of a hill one night, he called and called, but Y-yo-ha-rivg-nain did not answer him. Then he cried with such wild terrible pleading in his voice that Y-yo-ha-rivg-nain decided to respond.

" 'Itaru,' He said, and His voice sounded like the thunder that comes just after Taquich[21] flashes his sharp fire across the heavens, 'go, Itaru, and put the ball of fire into the sky where it can give warmth and light to all people alike. When rest time comes I shall take it under my cloak so men can sleep, and when the people awake from their rest I shall put it back in the sky again.'

"Poor Itaru was so troubled that he was glad to put the great ball up in the sky where all alike could receive light and warmth from it, but the marks of his teeth can still be seen on the face of it. Ever since then Itaru talks to Y-yo-ha-rivg-nain alone in the night."

As the courier stopped talking, there was silence for a moment. Then the children sighed and stretched their legs and arms. The courier laughed, for after all it was a short story, and sometimes the Indian tales took hours, even days, to finish. He knew from the expressions on their faces that they wanted more but did not dare ask.

Puy-Puy turned around to get the warmth of the fire on his back and stuck his thin legs out in front of him. Suddenly he drew them up quickly and bounded to his feet. Startled, the children looked to see what had made Puy-Puy jump. There stood old Pul Maat. He had been standing unseen in the shadows of the great oak for no one knew how long.

Amid the silent staring of the children—for they all stood in awe of this old man—he advanced among them. Instantly the children rose to their feet but sat down again as he himself sat down and motioned to them to resume their places by the fire. He had a deerskin cloak about his shoulders and eagle feathers in a band about his head.

The band had been woven from the hair cut from the head of a dead magician and was supposed to give the wearer something of the character of its original owner.

Puy-Puy was the last to sit down, and when he did, he sat as far away from Pul Maat as he could. Puy-Puy was a bit afraid of the wise man, because Puy-Puy did not always do just what was honest and fair, and he was afraid that Pul Maat would discover it through some of his magic ways.

"Now," said Pul Maat, "I will tell you another story of Itaru—why he runs away and is afraid of the river." He took the little black plug out of the end of the tobacco cane which ran through the lobe of his ear but found the cane empty, so he put the plug back. The children were glad that he was not going to smoke. He was called Pul Maat, the wise man of the smoke, because he could talk to the spirits of the dead through the wreaths of smoke he blew from his pipe. They all believed him when he said he could do this, and it frightened the children.

"Itaru could run very fast," said Pul Maat. "He had a way of getting out of sight so quickly that no one could find where he had gone. Because he could do this he was very proud of himself. All the other animals thought he was too proud. He made them dislike him by bragging, where they could all hear him, about his fast running.

"One day he bragged too much. The other animals, the bear, the mountain lion, the wolf, the deer, the antelope, and the mountain sheep heard him and looked at each other with sly winks. Itaru saw these and got reckless with his bragging. Even the river laughed as it rippled over its bed.

"Itaru heard that laugh and, running to the bank, said scornfully, 'I can run faster than you can, O Wenot!'

"Wenot, the river, said not a word. It just ran along babbling and laughing to itself. The other animals did not say a word, either; they waited to see what Itaru would do.

" 'I shall run a race with you, Wenot,' said Itaru to the river. 'It will not be hard to run faster than you do, for you are very slow.'

"You can see how foolishly proud Itaru was, for it is not always that the river runs slowly; sometimes it washes away its banks it goes so swiftly.

"Now the river did not like Itaru, but it said, in its pleasant, rippling way, 'Very well, I shall race with you.'

"Giving the river one scornful glance, Itaru began to run. He ran along the riverbank. He ran so fast that the other animals gave up trying to keep pace with him and sat down to wait for him to return.

"Itaru ran until he was tired, and then, looking over the riverbank, he saw the river running along beside him. He could see it stretching way out before him running and laughing on its way to the sea.

"So Itaru ran again. He ran faster this time until his tongue hung out of his mouth and his legs ached as he ran. His breath came in short gasps.

" 'I'll beat the old river this time,' he panted to himself, as he raced around a bend in the river-bank. But when he went to the edge of the river, there was the river running along as quietly as before. Nor could he see any of it behind him, for the bend shut it off from his view. It was all ahead of him, stretched way out wide and long across the plains to the sea. It was not even tired.

"Itaru took a deep breath and ran faster and faster. He ran until he was so tired he had to stop and lie down. But the river ran on past him.

"Then Itaru knew that Wenot, the river, had won the race. He had run as fast as he could, and still the river ran ahead of him, untired, quiet, and strong. Itaru walked off with his tail between his tired legs.

"How the other animals laughed at him! Every time he saw the river it gurgled and laughed at him, too, and so Itaru did not like the river any more, nor did he feel so proud. In fact, that is why he slinks about with all his pride gone and is not like other animals. Now, when he sees the river, he always puts his tail between his legs and runs away from it. The river did not ever stop. It has been running ever since on its way to the sea."

Pul Maat got to his feet, and all the children respectfully rose also and were careful not to pass between him and any one of the others, or between him and the fire, for this would show a disobedient and disrespectful attitude. No one in his right mind ever showed disrespect to any member of the *Puplum*, especially old Pul Maat.

"*Yamu uimi*, I am going," he said to the courier, who answered the usual word, "*Mea*, go!" Nor was this curtness disrespectful; it was the Indian way.

The children knew the storytelling was over, and each one scampered away in the dark to crawl into his own wickiup and dream of Itaru, the fiery ball, and the running water.

Crawled into his wickiup.

# 6

# Yamino-Kwiti Meets Itaru

ONE SUMMER MORNING Yamino-Kwiti left the village and went along the river trail toward the mountains. He was not happy, and like most people when they are not happy he wanted to be alone.

His unhappiness had started the night before when his father told him that Pul Maat and Siba-vik had definitely decided to select him for the *Yobagnar*. Pul Maat had been observing him for some time, and he and Siba-vik felt that Yamino-Kwiti would make a good *Pul*. His instruction would begin immediately. He would be one of several children chosen for this severe training. He would have to remember, and repeat without error, all the legends and the traditions of his tribe, which were told from one generation to the next. This was the only way they knew of preserving their ancient knowledge.

Mamish-Ahikañ had explained all this to him, and with despair in his voice he had cried out, "But, Father! Can't I be a courier like you?" The corners of his mouth were drawn down in a woebegone expression of defeat.

Itaru did not like the river any more.

When he came to deep pools he swam through them.

His father was surprised at the deep feeling Yamino-Kwiti displayed and hesitated before he answered. He would like very much to have his son become a courier like himself, but the choice was not his.

Other Indians could run fast, too, although few were as fleet of foot as he himself, the courier of the chief. And Yamino-Kwiti had already earned his name, which meant "the running boy." He had no sooner learned to walk when a baby than he began to run and with infant glee had run away from his mother and his grandmother. So they called him "Yamino-Kwiti." But it was not because of his running that he had attracted the attention of the *Puplum*. It was because there were few of the Indian boys who were as bright and quick as the son of the courier.

Pul Maat had told them all, "He will make a good *Pul* if trained early."

"Why do you want to be a courier, Yamino-Kwiti?" asked his father.

"Because, my father, I want to see the places you have seen, and go where you have gone. I want to see Momáti, the ocean, and the mountain where lives Taquich, the ball lightning, and Tauwaro, the thunder, and the great desert, and other people—the ones who build the great canoes,[22] and those who make the stone pots in the islands of Pimu."

He did not tell his father that he also wanted

to see the porpoises that circled around the edge of the world, nor the seven giants who held the world up on their shoulders, for fear he would say that Yamino-Kwiti could not go, and so he repeated only the places where his father himself had gone.

"I understand," said his father slowly. "Perhaps, if the Elders of the Council realize what a good runner you are, they will change their decision, but I do not think so. You will have to do as they say, for when you grow tall and manly, it is the chief and the council you obey, not me."

Yamino-Kwiti knew he would have to obey. He could not forget that once when he was a very little boy there had been another Indian child who misbehaved so continually that he had been slain. He could remember vividly the ruthless certainty of the arrows that ended his rebellious, defiant existence. The parents of that child had left the village and with their possessions had gone, no one knew where, rather than stay and be disgraced all the rest of their lives because they had had a child who could not obey. Yes, he would have to obey.

With a heavy heart Yamino-Kwiti took his throwing stick and his bow and arrows and headed in the direction of the big mountains. Tamít, the sun, was well above the edge of the world shining brightly in the hazy blue of his trail, and Yamino-Kwiti was a long way from the village. He climbed up on the limb of a sycamore and looked about him.

In this month when the young eagles fly, the

blackberry vines were blossoming along the river-
banks. Wild roses with their fragile, pink petals
and sweet fragrance abounded everywhere. The
wild grapevines hung in blossoming festoons
among the trees. The fireflowers, or golden poppies, still spread a shimmering fire mantle over
the slopes—so bright and gay a sight that even
the Indians at the shore marveled at its brightness. The river ran wide and full over its round
boulders and pebbles toward the sea. There were
tall, rustling sycamores, pussy willows, and cottonwood trees along its banks, and sturdy live-oaks
spreading wide branches among the brush.

Yamino-Kwiti could no longer see the village
with its rounded mat huts and willow-pole *Yoba*,
and a feeling of loneliness came over him. The
Indian boys seldom went far afield alone, and even
the older men hunted in pairs. There were too
many tales of danger about Hunar, the great bear,
Icauvut, the wolf, Cut, the rattlesnake, and Tukut,
the panther. These were, he knew, things with
which to be reckoned. He was rebellious and disappointed and wanted in some way to show the
Elders of the Council that he would make a better
hunter or courier than he would a *Pul*. All the
members of the *Puplum* filled him with awe, and
even fear, especially old Pul Maat, who saw the
spirits of the dead in his smoke clouds.

He was not certain how he was to accomplish
his great deeds of daring, but it had seemed the

most natural thing in the world to go toward the mountains. He had walked a long, long time, and although the village was nowhere in sight, the mountains seemed as far away as ever.

He sat high on the limb of the tree and swung his bare feet, watching the morning shadows grow shorter with each passing moment. A meadow lark sang its clear, silvery song not far away, just as it does for us in the spring, and Yamino-Kwiti lifted his head to listen to its call. Larks were good to eat.

A little rabbit sat up on his haunches to look inquiringly at the bare, brown feet hanging down from the limb of the tree, but when Yamino-Kwiti —more from habit than from any need of food at the moment—raised his throwing stick, the rabbit was too quick for him and disappeared into a near-by hole. Its little white knob of a tail was like a flash of light down the darkness of its burrow.

Suddenly he heard something moving in the brush, something he could not see! He was glad he had not thrown his throwing stick at the rabbit, but had it still in his hand. He watched expectantly, hoping it would be Shukat, the deer, who would raise his horns above the tops of the brush.

If he could kill Shukat, the deer, now! And he pictured himself dragging a dead deer into the village for all to praise him for his youthful skill. The big bows and arrows which the men used for large game were too large for him, and his own bow and arrows were too small to kill Shukat. Perhaps if it were a very small deer, he thought, he could use his throwing stick and bring Shukat to earth. He did not realize that his eagerness to do big deeds was causing him to dream wild dreams.

Instead of the horns of Shukat moving in the brush, he saw two yellow eyes peering at him from the ground. He saw Itaru, the coyote, with his gaunt, tawny body and gray belly. Yamino-Kwiti was glad that he was in the tree. Itaru was not anywhere near as large as Hunar, or as Shukat, or Tukut, the panther, and Itaru did not attack men. He talked in the moonlight with the Giver of Life, and Yamino-Kwiti had heard it said that the wise men of the *Puplum* were sometimes counseled by Itaru. Itaru was wise among animals, and Yamino-Kwiti was awed by the sight of him so near.

Perhaps, Yamino-Kwiti thought, perhaps Itaru would give him counsel now. So he leaned down from his perch in the tree and said in a hushed voice, "Itaru! O Itaru, will you help me to be a courier? Will you tell Pul Maat that I shall make a good courier—a much, much better courier than I would a *Pul?*"

Itaru did not answer. Slowly, with his yellow eyes fixed on Yamino-Kwiti, he withdrew his gaunt body into the underbrush. He made no sound. He was gone!

Yamino-Kwiti listened, then he called softly: "Itaru! Itaru!" But Itaru did not answer. There was no sound anywhere. Even the quail and the meadow lark, knowing that their enemy was near at hand, did not call or sing. The chaparral, even, did not move, for the breeze which had been so fresh in the early morning was gone now. Nothing stirred.

Yamino-Kwiti began to be afraid. Why had Itaru not answered him? Didn't he want Yamino-Kwiti to be a courier, either? Then Yamino-Kwiti felt as though all the world were against him. He was more keenly disappointed than ever. He wanted now to go home, for Itaru's silence and the stillness all about him had dampened his enthusiasm. He who had been so daring in his own village now felt very small and alone. He was in awe of the uncanny presence of Itaru, who was, according to tradition, a supernatural creature.

He looked about him and saw the river flowing along, and then he remembered the story that Pul Maat had told the boys about Itaru. If Itaru were afraid of the river, Yamino-Kwiti would wade down the river to the village!

He jumped up and down on the limb of the tree, making the branches crackle and swish. He yelled at the top of his voice, "I am calling! Itaru! I am going, Itaru!"

Scrambling down from his perch in the tree, he ran as fast as his bare feet could take him down the bank to the river. He waded out into the cool stream as it rippled over rocks and shallows. Here he stopped his yelling and breathed freely again, watching his steps in the current of the river. When big boulders obstructed his path and made waterfalls, he climbed the bank and ran along as Itaru himself had done in the story. When he came to deep pools he swam through them, the current carrying him along.

Tamít, the sun, was high in the sky when Yamino-Kwiti saw the village. Wushi came running to meet him. Wushi did not bark as the other dogs did, but trotted silently until he met Yamino-Kwiti. Long ago one of Yamino-Kwiti's forefathers had tamed a wolf cub, and he was the ancestor of Wushi, who was part wolf even yet. He seldom barked, but sometimes howled, especially at night when distant cousins of his, the wolves and the coyotes, filled the night air with their restless yowling. Then all the dogs in the village of Siba would answer and make the night clamorous.

Yamino-Kwiti's mother saw him coming. She stood gravely watching him as he approached. "Ah, Little Runner," she said, "I thought you had gone with the men, brave little thing that you are."

Of course Yamino-Kwiti felt ashamed. He had gone forth to prove his ability as a hunter and had been afraid, instead.

"Mother," he said, "I am not brave—I was afraid of Itaru. I ran down the river to get home, because Itaru is afraid of the river."

His mother laughed at him. "Itaru does not hurt little boys. Come," she told him, "there is something for you to do. Pul Maat has been asking for you. Many, many things you must learn yet, Yamino-Kwiti, before you can go wandering alone again," and she shook her head at him.

During the weeks that followed, Yamino-Kwiti sat with Pul Maat under the spreading oak tree near his hut for a little while each morning. He was not told the secrets which he wanted to hear —not yet, for he must be trained in other things to test his memory first. He sat very still while Pul Maat talked to him, but he wanted to squirm and wriggle, for Pul Maat made him uncomfortable just as the old Pul Tauwaro used to do before he died. The two old men were very much alike, and although Yamino-Kwiti listened attentively to all that Pul Maat said to him, there were moments when he wondered if Pul Maat would come back and be a bear, too, after he died. His voice was deep and growly, even now, just as Pul Tauwaro's used to be. This thought caused him to make a mistake when Pul Maat asked him to repeat what he had just heard.

He was always glad when Pul Maat said he might go, and he got up and ran like a deer to join the other boys, hoping with all his heart that somehow he would not be considered fit for the *Yobagnar*. He wanted more than ever to be a courier like his father, even though he knew the other boys envied him the honor the *Puplum* had conferred on him. He knew, too, that really he had no choice in the matter.

Throwing stick or "makanas," and time-beating stick.

# 7

# The Prophecy of Muhut

WARM BREEZE blew across the little village of Siba. Down in the shallow pools by the river where the water grasses grew tall and thick, the frogs had set up a noisy chorus of croaking. "Gr-gr-oik-oik, groik, oik, groik-oik," sang the frogs, but the excited clamor that rose from a whole village of Indians drowned the frog chorus.

"The frogs! The frogs!" they called back and forth to each other. "Summer has come! The cold wind and the rain have returned to the north!"

The old folks about the village smiled contentedly, for they found each winter a little colder than the last for their old bones. They were grateful for the warm sunshine of summer which had been heralded by the frogs, big and little.

The medicine man had cured Grandfather of his burns, and that lively old man went about his activities as usual, but Grandmother had not recovered. When Yamino-Kwiti went to her hut he could hear the medicine man inside. He was saying over and over some incantation which Yamino-Kwiti could not understand, and each verse ended with *"Nom im manoc, im manoc; nom im manoc, im manoc; Yobarse!"* What he actually said was, "What I do, I do; what I do, I do; O sacred Place!" What he meant was, "I do this in the name of the Giver of Life!"

Yamino-Kwiti did not dare interrupt the medicine man, so he crept silently away and waited until he saw the old man leave the hut. Then he went to his grandmother.

"How are you today, my old one?" he asked.

She smiled slowly and put her thin old hand out to touch his black hair. "Not so well, Little Runner." And then, because he looked so distressed, she added with a smile, "Even a long trail must end, Yamino-Kwiti, and mine has been a long one." She did not know that the boy held a secret in his heart that weighed heavily upon his spirits. He was thinking of the prophecy of Muhut, the owl.

One morning Grandmother did not waken. Her long, long sleep had begun. All the relatives—and there were many of them: sons and daughters, grandchildren, nephews and nieces, cousins and more cousins—began their mourning almost immediately. Amid lamentations they cut their hair. The closest of kin cut it shortest; the others, the cousins, merely clipped it. Even Yamino-Kwiti's and Puku-Kakar's was cut. The courier, his brothers, and their wives all cut their long, black hair off short, and Grandfather's scraggy white poll was cropped closer than any of them, since he was the most bereaved. Yamino-Kwiti hardly knew his mother when he saw her with all her long black hair cut short.

Wailing and crying, moaning and groaning were begun while preparations went on for the ceremony of the dead. Each mourner had his own peculiar groan or wail. It made a weird chorus at which even Itaru might marvel.

All the belongings of Grandmother were gathered together and put in a large basket: her sea-otter cape, her pretty shell beads, her favorite mortar with its basket hopper and its worn pestle, her bone awls made from bird-wing bones with

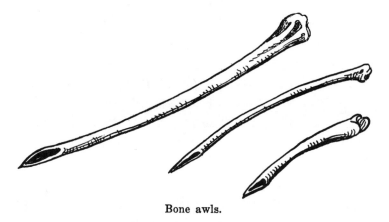

Bone awls.

which she sewed, the beautiful large abalone shell with its little holes stopped up with bitumen from the Tar Pits[23] down near Yangna[8]—all these had been treasures of Grandmother and were to be burned with her body on the funeral pyre. Even her pot of steatite,[24] which she had treasured, had a hole punched in its bottom to show it had not survived its owner and was never to be used again.

"We must have more feathers for the *Yobagnar*," said the mother of Puku-Kakar to Yamino-Kwiti's mother as they gathered these things together, each moaning in a different key.

"Yes, we need more," was the answer, "many more, but who will get them?"

"Mother," said Yamino-Kwiti, "I will get the feathers."

His mother sat back on her heels and paused in her work. "You? Why, yes, you go get some feathers."

He called Puku-Kakar, and leaving all the wailing and moaning behind them they took their throwing sticks and went out into the chaparral.

"Let us get the beautiful long feathers of Panes, the condor,"[25] said Puku-Kakar, who had been very fond of his grandmother and felt that the very best and biggest feathers he could get to put before Kwawar in the *Yobagnar* would not be fine enough. "I know how to catch them," he added.

Yamino-Kwiti said nothing, for he, too, had watched the capture of vultures, eagles, and condors, whose feathers were so important in the making of ceremonial skirts and headdresses as well as for decorations in the *Yobagnar* in mourning rites.

With throwing sticks in their hands they made their way to the north. Between the village of

Siba and the mountains were miles of chaparral
where lived many a small animal and even some
of the larger ones like the deer, the antelope, the
small brown bear, and many of the coyote's brothers and cousins.

Here a rabbit-hunt fire had burned a large area,
leaving it bare save for the blackened twigs of
the shrubs. A fierce, dry wind had carried the fire
past the Indians' control. They had, however,
made the most of it, for after the fire had died
down they found many roasted grasshoppers, insects, and small animals, which they ate with relish
just as they found them.

Into this burned area the boys made their way.
They caught and killed several rabbits and took
them along. These they placed on the ground in
the center of the clearing and lay down beside
them, faces toward the sky. No restless white boy
could have lain as still as long as these two Indian
boys. Not a move did they make, although the
ants and other insects crawled over them in great
numbers.

Up in the blue dome above them floated a few
thin clouds, but there was something else besides
the clouds that the boys watched expectantly—a
wee black speck which circled and grew larger.
Soon there were more black specks. The boys could
see them growing larger and larger as they
wheeled and glided and came nearer and nearer.

Neither boy spoke nor moved, but each grasped

the throwing stick in his hand more tightly and waited, silently, motionless.

The vultures came nearer, hovering above, watching with wary eyes the motionless figures lying supine upon the ground like dead things. Had either boy moved a single muscle the birds would have flown on, seeking their feast elsewhere. Yamino-Kwiti and Puku-Kakar watched through half-closed eyelids as the birds alighted near them, stepping cautiously, turning their heads this way and that, ready at the slightest motion to take wing again. Not a sign of life was there in either boy. Well they knew their eyes would be the first juicy morsel selected by these ruthless scavengers as the first tidbit for their meal. The boys' hands grasped their weapons with every nerve ready for a swift stroke.

The dead rabbits beside them were the first objects attacked by the wary eye snatchers, and still the boys did not move, for up in the blue sky, rapidly sailing down, down, on long graceful wings, was one of the largest condors the boys had ever seen. Could they lie still long enough so as not to frighten the vultures away? Should there be even a motion toward flight by them, the condor, too, would glide away.

None too soon the great bird landed with a rustle of feathers from his enormous wings. The group of vultures pecking at the dead rabbits, still a bit wary of the two motionless bodies of the boys, scuttled aside as the condor approached, like vassals grudgingly giving way to the king at a feast.

With folded wings the huge bird strutted toward Yamino-Kwiti, who knew that he would have to be as swift as a striking snake, since these big birds had a way of thrusting their heads forward to peck with a startling quickness.

"Now!" shouted Puku-Kakar, just as Yamino-Kwiti raised his throwing stick and struck the condor on the head. As the two apparently dead figures came to life suddenly, there was a terrific beating of wings—huge wings—and dust flew in the air. Squawks and shrieks drowned the excited words of encouragement the boys gave one another as they struck and struck again.

In less than a moment the whole group of greedy birds were winging away in the blue with the exception of the condor and two vultures, whose feathered bodies lay at the feet of the youthful and excited hunters.

The boys were wild with excitement, for this was the first condor they had ever caught, and such a feat was work for a man. The enormous bird was a heavy load for Yamino-Kwiti, but with the help of Puku-Kakar he got it on his back and, after covering the weary miles through the chaparral, staggered into the village with Puku-Kakar in the lead bearing his two vultures. The numerous relatives of Grandmother were still filling the air with their wailing, but Yamino-Kwiti and Puku-

Kakar were too out of breath to take up their dirges just yet.

Yamino-Kwiti was as proud as the great bird itself when it perches on a high cliff and surveys the world at his feet. The *Puplum* forgot their sacred dignity and excitedly lifted the great bird, stretching out his wings to see the wide spread which, if they measured by their money strings, would be over six *ponko*. The red-orange, wrinkled skin of the bird's head had changed color with death and looked purplish and pale, but the black ruff about the neck was as glossy and black as ever, and the white patches under the wings showed only when the wings were spread out by the interested hands of the *Puplum*. The spots of red feathers on the breast and each knee were pounced upon by the *Puplum* as the bits for the grave sticks. Yamino-Kwiti was glad, when he looked at the great strong hooked beak, that he had been too quick for the ruthless thing to peck out his eyes. He breathed a long sigh of relief and thankfulness that he had been able to bring such glorious feathers, some of which were two feet long, to decorate the *Yobagnar* for the funeral ceremony.

It had been a deed of brave effort and endurance for so small a boy to bring such a heavy burden so far across the rough trail. The childish body was utterly weary, but no one praised him for the feat of strength, nor did he expect it; their delight and wonder over the great bird itself was praise enough.

Wood had been gathered during his absence. In a shallow pit to the west of the village stood a great pile. The thin little body of the silent old woman was wrapped in her tule mat with some seeds, money, and food for her long journey into Tucupar, the heaven of the Indians, and was laid on the top of the pile. They had cut a lock of her hair which, with a few of her possessions, were to be put aside for the next ceremony in commemoration[26] of the dead, but her other possessions were to be burned with her that she might be well supplied in Tucupar.

Some of the distant relatives were appointed fire tenders and would be paid for their task. All but these individuals now withdrew into the *Yoba*, where they stayed during the burning of the pyre, singing and wailing and shuffling their feet in a melancholy sort of dance. When the cremation was ended, the fire tenders danced the fire dance, which gradually put out the fire. Every ember was trodden into the soil by those dancing feet, while inside the *Yoba*, songs were sung to words sorrowfully repeated over and over and ending with a shrill whistle made by blowing through the hollow tube of a deer's leg bone. Yamino-Kwiti was fascinated by this whistle and wondered, if they should make a *Pul* of him, if he could be the chief whistler. It was the only part of any ceremony which he had as yet witnessed that had appealed to him.

After many days the ceremony composed of dances, songs, and feasts had ended, and life in the village resumed its regular, lazy, good-natured rhythm. Then Yamino-Kwiti told his mother of the prophecy of Muhut, the owl.

"Why did you not tell us of it?" she asked him.

"I thought, perhaps, if no one else knew it, it might not come true," he said.

"But, my Little Runner," she told him, "even if you had not heard it, the *nanah*, the leaves which are the ears of the trees, heard it."

Yamino-Kwiti had nothing to say to that but looked up at the leaves of the cottonwood before him and saw them trembling in the wind. Yes, the leaves of the trees were their ears. They heard everything, for Ahikañ, the wind, told them all that went on in the air and on the earth. But they never, never told anything to an Indian, although they whispered continually to one another.

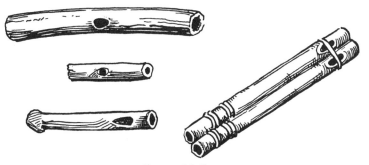

Bone whistles.

# 8

# The Boy with the Crooked Toe

**J**UST ABOVE the village of Siba was a place where the river narrowed and fell over a big boulder into a pool. For untold ages the running water had dug deeper and deeper until the pool was deep and wide. In the shadows of overhanging trees the trout hid.

The sunlight filtered through the willows that lined the banks and fell on the black head of a small Indian boy. He was sitting very still, the very picture of dejection. Even the corners of his mouth were drawn down, and although there were no tears in his eyes, it appeared as though there might, be any moment. He was so still that the trout came out from the shadows in the pool and nibbled at his toes as they dangled limp and motionless in the water.

Suddenly a big splash in front of him made him jump, and the trout flashed into their sheltering nooks. The widening ripples on the surface of the water told the story of a stone thrown in. Yamino-Kwiti looked about him, aware that there was someone else in the quiet place, but he could see no one. He got up from the rock on which he was sitting and, looking about him, finally called, "Who's there?"

Someone laughed—a small rippling giggle—and Yamino-Kwiti shouted, "I know! It's Kihut-Kiur!"*

On the other side of the pool Kihut-Kiur stood laughing. She put her two little hands together and dived into the water. Pulling herself up on the rock where Yamino-Kwiti stood, she said, "What were you thinking about, Yamino-Kwiti? You sat so still one would think you were asleep."

"I wasn't asleep. I was thinking about Pul Maat."

Kihut-Kiur shivered. "I don't like him. I'm afraid of him. His voice rumbles and he frowns at me as though he were angry."

"It isn't that," said Yamino-Kwiti. "I'm not afraid of him, but he makes me learn all sorts of things and repeat them to him. He doesn't want me to be a courier—and I want to be a courier."

"Why do you want to be a courier, Yamino-Kwiti?" asked the little girl, who had been taught that it was a great privilege to be trained for the *Yobagnar*.

"Because," said Yamino-Kwiti, "my father is a courier, and he knows all about the rest of the world. He goes into the desert and knows the desert people; he goes to the mountains from where the thunder comes, and he goes to the sea and even

---

* Kee-hoot'-Kee-oor'.

to the islands out in the ocean. I want to go to those places and see the things my father has told me about. I don't want to be in the *Yobagnar*, dancing and singing all the time—I don't like the *Puplum!*" And Yamino-Kwiti stamped his foot, not at all like an obedient little Indian boy.

"Oh, Yamino-Kwiti, you'd better not say that where they can hear you! Or Pul Maat had better not, either."

"They'll not hear me—but what can I do, Kihut-Kiur?"

Kihut-Kiur thought a moment and then said brightly, "I'll tell you, Yamino-Kwiti! They're just testing you out now, and if they found out that you were the very best runner in the village and that you did not have a good memory and forgot what they taught you——"

Yamino-Kwiti interrupted her. "But to be a courier I have to have a *very good* memory. If I forgot what they teach me now, then they'll say I won't be a good courier, either."

The two children were silent for a moment. It did not seem very hopeful. But there must be some way out, thought Kihut-Kiur.

"I'll tell you, Yamino-Kwiti. Suppose you practice running, every day, until you are the strongest and swiftest runner of them all. Then when the time comes for you to be initiated into the *Yobagnar*, the chief will want you for a courier instead."

Little did either of them know how both his

There was a terrific beating of wings as they struck and struck
again.

A huge form presented itself on the trail.

running and his excellent memory were to serve
him in another summer.

"It won't be long now," said Yamino-Kwiti.
"They have begun to teach me the dance steps
already; ugh, I'd rather run!"

"Come," said Kihut-Kiur, "there is no time to
lose. Let us begin racing right now!"

They left the pool and went where the trail
turned away from the river. Between the villages
of Asuksa and Siba, after crossing the miry places,
they came to a broad, flat stretch on the trail.
Here they began their running.

Every day found them there, Kihut-Kiur doing
her part in racing with Yamino-Kwiti and urging
him on. Always he left her far behind, panting
and puffing, but she did not mind and only threw
herself down on the grass and laughed. *"Alala!*[27]
Yamino-Kwiti," she said, "you get farther ahead
of me every day!"

Each time Yamino-Kwiti lengthened his run
until he found his path getting almost into the
Asuksa territory, where it narrowed a bit between
tall bushes of manzanita and wild lilac. He was
running more easily now, and longer, without los-
ing his breath, as he had done in the first days of
his practicing.

One day, however, as he went at his very best
speed, he rounded a turn in the trail and came
suddenly upon a wild grapevine tied across the
path. He was going too fast to stop, and all he

could do was to jump, and jump high, with a lift
of his entire body. Quickly he thought of Kihut-
Kiur coming along behind him, and instead of
continuing his run he turned and lifted the vine
so that when Kihut-Kiur came panting around the
turn she ran under it.

Then the two children stopped to consider why
that grapevine was there. "Who did it?" they
asked each other. Yamino-Kwiti looked about him,
and his quick glance discovered a strange footprint.

"Look, Kihut-Kiur! Look!" he whispered excitedly. It was the print of a boy's foot with a
crooked toe! Someone was trying to trip him—
but who? And why?

The children got down on their knees and examined the print until they would know it anywhere, and then they tried to see where it led.
But after tracking it along the trail a few paces
and down to the edge of the wash they lost it there.
The shadows were getting long from the west, so
they turned toward Siba, wondering who the enemy was who had tried to trip Yamino-Kwiti.

Several days after this incident, Yamino-Kwiti
and the little girl were again running their races.
They no longer went into Asuksa territory but
followed the trail by the river. Three times Yamino-Kwiti had run the pace, when a long willow
pole was suddenly thrust out from the bushes at
the side of the path, and down went Yamino-
Kwiti. He had been going so fast that the fall

sent him headfirst into a bed of nettles from which he got up, his naked brown body tingling all over. His knee was badly skinned, too. Then came Kihut-Kiur, running. "Oh, Yamino-Kwiti, what happened?"

"Someone tripped me with a long pole," he said through set teeth, for his knee smarted and the nettle pricks burned and stung. These he must not mind, for did not the hunters thus sting themselves before they went to hunt?

"Let's go down to the river," said Kihut-Kiur, and Yamino-Kwiti followed her, limping. There Kihut-Kiur found a broad, juicy leaf and laid it on the smarting, skinned knee, and taking up handfuls of mud from the edge of the river she applied it to all the stinging parts of his body. Yamino-Kwiti sighed, "That feels good. Put some more on." After all, he was not a hunter yet; there was enough time for the self-inflicted torture when he was of age to hunt with the men.

He was a funny-looking sight as they went slowly home, and Kihut-Kiur couldn't help laughing. Yamino-Kwiti laughed, too, for after all she had been very helpful in putting on the healing mud and the herb.

It was several days before Yamino-Kwiti's sore knee was well enough for him to return to his running. His mother, in applying fresh leaves to the wound, asked her small son many questions and discovered the resentment in the child's heart.

She, too, like Kihut-Kiur, encouraged him about his running, although she knew the great honor conferred upon him by the *Puplum*.

"You are as swift as a little deer when Itaru is after it," she said. "You would make a good courier."

As soon as his knee was well enough, Yamino-Kwiti and Kihut-Kiur went on an investigating tour. They intended to hunt for the print of the crooked toe and trace it to its owner, but they had not yet reached the big toyon-berry bush at the turn of the trail when they came face to face with a strange boy.

The three children stood looking at each other for a silent moment, and then Yamino-Kwiti's quick eye discovered that the bare toes of the other boy were digging into the dirt in an anxious manner, and that the big toe on his right foot was crooked!

"So?" he said, "you are the boy who tried to trip me?"

The boy sneered. "You think you can run!" He spoke with a great showing of contempt.

"Well, he can!" championed Kihut-Kiur. "He can run faster than anyone—he can run faster than Shukat, the deer, even!"

Again the boy sneered. He was not a pleasant sight when he sneered, for it twisted his face until it was very ugly. He said something under his breath which sounded to Yamino-Kwiti very much like *yayare*, which no Indian boy was allowed to say to another, especially to a girl.

"What did you say?" Yamino-Kwiti demanded, but the boy only sneered again.

"Now we shall see," said Kihut-Kiur, "who can run the faster—you or Yamino-Kwiti! We shall have a race right now!"

Unwillingly the boy toed the mark which Yamino-Kwiti drew across the path.

"*Pukú, wehé, páhe,*[28] go!" shouted Kihut-Kiur, and off the boys went. They had gone only a few paces when the strange boy spread his elbows and pushed Yamino-Kwiti into the bushes. Yamino-Kwiti narrowly avoided a fall, but caught himself and went on. This gave the strange boy an advantage, and he shot ahead. Here the trail narrowed and wound between tall bushes. Although Yamino-Kwiti caught up with the other he was not able to pass him. Nor was there anything to catch hold of, for the boy was as naked as he himself—nothing, except his hair, which flopped up and down as he ran.

Reaching out, Yamino-Kwiti caught hold of that tangled mat and yanked the boy back with a jerk. Down they both went in the dust of the trail, punching and battling and chattering excitedly. Kihut-Kiur clasped her hands tightly together and chattered as ably as the boys, but her chatter came to a sudden stop when a huge form presented itself on the trail. It was Hunar, the great bear!

The little girl gave a scream. The strange boy gave a gasp, and, gathering himself to his feet, he shot past Yamino-Kwiti and Kihut-Kiur so fast there was no doubt whatsoever as to his ability as a runner. He had no sooner passed Yamino-Kwiti than that young hero jumped between Kihut-Kiur and the greatly surprised and curious creature. Yamino-Kwiti spread out his arms in front of his playmate and looked Hunar in the eye.

Slowly Hunar rose on her hind legs, towering above the children like a veritable giant, but Yamino-Kwiti stood his ground with Kihut-Kiur trembling behind him.

"If you're old Pul Tauwaro," said Yamino-Kwiti, in as brave a voice as he could manage, "you know better than to scare little girls!"

For one awful moment Hunar regarded the chil-

Lifting hot stones into the water.

dren with an air of curiosity and surprise. Then, slowly turning on her hind legs, she dropped on all fours and ambled off in the direction from which she had come. This time Yamino-Kwiti had not run from Hunar, but Hunar had run from Yamino-Kwiti.

As the children returned to the village they decided to tell no one about the strange boy, or Hunar, for that might lead to questions about why they were there on the trail to Asuksa. Only Yamino-Kwiti's mother knew their secret.

# 9

# Yamino-Kwiti Is Left Behind

KOTI-CUIT sat down in the sunshine outside his hut but got up again very quickly, for the ground was hot. "*Ala-la!* The seven giants who hold up the earth must have built a fire down there," he said.

The other Indians, lying in the shade, all laughed. Some of them who lay on their backs kicked at the air, they laughed so hard. Yamino-Kwiti looked at his uncle and wondered if what he said were true. How could seven giants hold up the world and at the same time build a fire, he wondered. The only way he knew that a fire could be built was done by both hands whirling a stick in dry wood until a spark came. Koti-Cuit saw the solemn expression on Yamino-Kwiti's face and said, "What makes it so hot, Yamino-Kwiti, if there isn't a fire somewhere?"

"It must be that Tamít, the sun, has come closer, so we feel him more," he answered, "because the ground cools off at night when Tamít is gone, Koti-Cuit."

"That is true," said Koti-Cuit and looked admiringly at Yamino-Kwiti. The other Indians stopped laughing. Here was the child who was being trained for the *Puplum,* and he was already showing more wisdom than the older men.

"I think," said Siba-vik, "that we shall go to the shore tomorrow, where it will be cooler. We shall make a trading trip, and when we return to the village we shall have a winter's supply of sealskin, dried fish, and more stone pots."

"Let us not come back until it is cool enough to wear the sealskins, then," said one of the men.

"Yes, yes!" responded the others, and there was more loud laughter. The Indians were always merry and ready to laugh loudly at anything, like happy children.

At the thought of going to the shore, Yamino-Kwiti got up and ran to his father. He was not going to miss a chance to see the world if he could help it.

"Father," he said, "the men are going to the shore tomorrow. Am I to go, too?" He could not keep the eagerness out of his voice, and he almost held his breath waiting for his father's answer.

"We shall have to ask Pul Maat," answered the courier, "and if he says not, then you must be content and do as he says."

Yamino-Kwiti said nothing, but he did not feel very cheerful about his chance of going with the party. He knew the stern, surly nature of the old man who taught him to repeat and remember every word that was said to him, every dance step, and every song.

Very early the next morning his father woke Yamino-Kwiti and said, "Get up, Little Runner. The people are getting ready to go to Shua[8] by the sea."

"Am I going, too?" Yamino-Kwiti questioned eagerly.

"I am sorry, my son, but Pul Maat says not. The people will be gone for the rest of the Brown and Sear Moon[12] and even until the Gray Goose Moon.[12] During that time you are to practice your memory tests and other things which Pul Maat will give you to do. And you are to do as you are told."

Yamino-Kwiti could hear the crier going from hut to hut and calling, "Hear ye! The traders are going to Shua!" So he crawled through the little, low doorway into the open. It was still dark. The stars were paling, and the people of the village were moving about in the dark, making fires and preparing breakfasts. There was bustle and excitement all around, but Yamino-Kwiti was not happy as he moved slowly among them.

He watched the women making up bundles of deerskins, antelope skins, and the soft, tawny skins of the wildcat, while the young girls filled baskets with piñon nuts, chia seeds, and the large acorns from the mountains. These they put into carrying nets which the women bore on their backs, the bands of the nets across their foreheads protected by little basket caps. They would follow the men

and would bring back, in the same way, the island-
ers' fish, sea-otter skins, and soapstone bowls and
pots. Nor was this all they would bring back with
them, for it was at the shore that they found the
clams, and the little olivella shells that made such
beautiful necklaces. The rocks which were washed
over with waves at high tide yielded abalones when
the tide was low. Then, too, there were those little
bits of black *sanot*,[29] or asphaltum, found all along
the beach, which they used to make their baskets
watertight, and to stop up the little holes in the
abalone shells so they could use them for bowls.

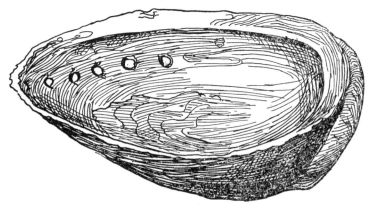

Abalone shells were used for various purposes. With the holes
plugged with asphalt they were used for bowls and scoops.

There was much to be brought back from the shore,
and the women would come home with their carrying nets full laden. If they bartered well they
would have longer strings of money beads to hang
around their necks, for it was thus they carried
their wealth.

It was an exciting and important expedition, and those who were to go strutted about feeling superior. The chief's courier said good-by to his family and left, not waiting for the rest of the party. It was his task to announce the coming of the tribe to the shore where the people from Pimu brought their goods for barter. Because he ran, not only as naked as the others, but with no provisions or weapons whatsoever, and the message carried only in his memory, they called him Mamish-Ahikañ, or "the unencumbered one who goes like the wind."

It was barely light when the party left. Some of the older children went, too, for Indian children learn very early to be useful and a part of the community. It was neither Yamino-Kwiti's nor Kihut-Kiur's good fortune to go. The little girl stood with her baby brother who hung on her back, still asleep in his willow basket. Stooping a bit under the burden, she watched the party leave. She wanted very much to go, and her little brown face was wistful and pensive. "I know now," she told herself, "how Yamino-Kwiti feels when they make him sit in the *Yoba* when he wants to go hunting with the other boys."

Yamino-Kwiti walked a little way with the party beside his uncle, Koti-Cuit. "Will you see the canoes," he asked his uncle, "and the men who make them? And the big fish—the fish that are as big as I am?"

The seven giants who hold up the earth.

Yamino-Kwiti walked a little way beside his uncle.

"Some of the fish are bigger than you are, Yamino-Kwiti," answered his uncle.

Yamino-Kwiti wondered about those big fish. The only ones he had seen were the minnows and trout in the river, none of which were much larger than a man's two hands. The women used to catch the fish by taking the amole[30] root and beating it in the pools until the water was soapy and foamy. Then the fish would come to the surface of the pool stupefied and were easily caught. If the ocean were as large as his father said it was, could they catch fish that way there?

"Can you find enough amole root, Koti-Cuit," he asked his uncle, "to catch the big fish?" Koti-Cuit laughed so hard he stopped on the trail and slapped his knees with his hands. Yamino-Kwiti felt so sheepish he ran back to the village without learning how Koti-Cuit caught the big fish.

All through the long, hot days that followed the departure of the traders, Yamino-Kwiti went on with his training. Sometimes, in the *Yoba* built for the young students, he and the other children would try to learn the dance steps for the ceremonies. First, they had to lift one foot and bring it down with a definite stamp, then the other foot twice lightly, then make a jump backward, and continue until perspiration ran from their small bodies like water. He envied Puku-Kakar, who was often sent on errands from village to village, as a young courier, like the father of Yamino-

Kwiti. Puku-Kakar could run like a deer, while
Yamino-Kwiti imitated wearily the steps of the
bear and the other animals in the dances, ending
each dance with a bearlike roar. Yamino-Kwiti
put his whole heart into the roar and made each
one loud and long. Pul Maat was pleased. He
thought Yamino-Kwiti was beginning to like the
*Yoba*. Little did he know that Yamino-Kwiti was
really voicing a protest when he roared, and it was
the only part of the training that he liked.

Plank canoe.

# 10

# The Bag of Magic and the Kidnappers

NE DAY a medicine man from Asuksa came into Siba and sat in the hut with A-nub-su-voi-rot. They smoked their pipes and talked in low tones, and then the medicine man went away.

All the rest of the afternoon and the next day, A-nub-su-voi-rot was busy. He went into the fields and came back with herbs and worked in his hut far into the night by the light of his fire which burned in a hole in the center of the floor. He was making magic.

The next day Puku-Kakar was told by A-nub-su-voi-rot to take a small deerskin packet, tied round and round with agave[31] fiber, to the medicine man at Asuksa. He was to go as quickly as he could, starting immediately, for the bag contained a magical cure for a sick woman—the wife of Asuksa-vik.

Tomear decided that he and the other boys, Wupu-Yatcho, Puy-Puy, and Yamino-Kwiti would follow after Puku-Kakar, and then all would go hunting. Since Puku-Kakar was to run without encumbrance the other boys carried his weapons. They followed the bank of the river where there

was a well-worn trail and loitered, as boys will,
eating manzanita berries on the way.

At Asuksa, the village dogs barked loudly as the
boys approached. The medicine man came with
the chief and others to meet them. Puku-Kakar
was nowhere to be seen. After a few questions
and answers had flown back and forth they discovered that Puku-Kakar had not reached Asuksa.

"Something has happened to him," said Yamino-
Kwiti to Tomear.

"We shall find him," Tomear said to the curious
and wondering crowd of villagers standing about.

Back they went on the trail, watching the path
for any signs of disturbance. They had traveled
in this way for a little while when they noticed
that the bushes at the side of the path were broken.
Getting down on his knees, Yamino-Kwiti examined the footprints and saw the one that had so
puzzled Kihut-Kiur and himself the day they had
been tripped on this same trail. It was the print
of a foot with a crooked toe. There were other
footprints, too.

They lost these among the brush, and, hunt as
they would in a widening circle, they could not
pick them up again. They were beginning to feel
baffled, when suddenly Yamino-Kwiti saw a thin
streamer of smoke coming from some trees in an
arroyo. He called the other boys together, and
they headed in the direction of the smoke.

The people of the valley in which lay Siba were

related among themselves, with only family quarrels to mar the peace between them, but there were common enemies who had occasionally made themselves known and felt. Those Indians of the far mountains to the east, and in the great desert beyond,[32] were much to be dreaded. There had been no war with them in the years of Yamino-Kwiti's life, but he and all the boys knew there had been wars and there were likely to be again. They knew, too, that prisoners of war were cruelly tortured and killed—this was the way they treated their own prisoners—and that the women were sometimes killed but more often were taken captive. So they were taught from earliest childhood to be always alert and wary.

Not knowing what they would find at the place of the smoke, they went cautiously and silently with bows and arrows ready. The smoke led them to the edge of the arroyo. The four boys crouched among the bushes behind some rocks and cautiously peeked to see what the smoke meant.

In the bed of the almost dry creek they saw Puku-Kakar tied to a tree. There were three other Indians there, and Yamino-Kwiti recognized one of them as the boy who had tripped him on the trail, another as the prisoner who had escaped, and the third as the man with many rings on his fingers. The first two were the ones who had burned the hut of Koti-Cuit, father of Puku-Kakar. The little package of magic which Puku-Kakar had carried lay on the sand between them. They were arguing about opening it.

"I told you that it is magic," said Puku-Kakar, twisting his hands in the strands that bound him, "and if you open it you will have bad fortune all the rest of your days." This statement made an impression on the captors, and they hesitated about opening the little deerskin packet. On a crotched stick a skinned rabbit was cooking over the fire. The men were unaware of anyone watching them.

Motioning to his companions to withdraw quietly, Yamino-Kwiti drew the boys away from the bushes which hid them.

"Listen," he whispered. "You three stay here and watch. I am going to circle around behind Puku-Kakar. When you hear the quail call three times throw stones down on those fellows to attract their attention. Then I shall cut Puku-Kakar loose. We shall run for the brush and wait for you to join us. As soon as you throw the stones you will run down the creekbank and cross just beyond the bend. We'll be waiting for you on the other side."

Quietly the boys waited. In a few moments they heard the call of the quail. They counted the three calls softly, "*pukú, wehé, páhe*," and noticed that Puku-Kakar raised his head and listened, too, for it was the call he and Yamino-Kwiti had always used between them. Instantly the boys threw stones at the three Indians who were squatting in the sand of the creekbed arguing and cooking. They bounded to their feet and looked in the direction from which the stones came. At the same time Yamino-Kwiti slipped behind the tree and cut the bonds from Puku-Kakar. True to his trust, the young courier grabbed the small bag from under the very noses of the surprised Indians and slipped into the bushes behind him before they could stop him. With apparent enemies on both sides of them, the three Indians did not know which way to go, so they took to their heels up the creekbed to find shelter behind some boulders. That gave Yamino-Kwiti and his friends the start they needed.

"I must take the packet to Asuksa," said Puku-Kakar as soon as they were all together.

"We shall all go," said Tomear, "for it was Asuksa men who kidnapped you."

They were all good runners, and now there was more incentive for hurry than before. When they arrived in the village of Asuksa, the chief, Asuksa-vik, stood beside the medicine man, and Tomear, as eldest son of the chief of Siba, became spokesman for the group.

"Siba-vik, my father, will talk with you," he said to Asuksa-vik. "These men of your village have waylaid a courier from Siba. They have made trouble before, but my father is away at Shua by the sea, and when he returns he will talk with you."

"Yes, we shall talk," answered Asuksa-vik.

It was late when the boys returned to Siba, and they had much to talk about as they ate their delayed dinner. They related all that had happened to Pul Sacasca-Tatma, who said they had acted like grown men, which pleased them. They called him Pul Sacasca-Tatma because he had one blue tooth right in the front of his mouth.

The warm days passed quickly, and soon it was cooler and time for the traders to return. This event was eagerly awaited by all of the villagers. Yamino-Kwiti and Puku-Kakar were eager to tell their fathers of the latest insult from the family enemies at Asuksa.

One night, when Moar, the moon, was as big and round as the top of the water basket, Mamish-Ahikañ came panting into the village. "The party will be here tomorrow," he said, "with many, many things."

After he had been fed and rested he told the eager listeners about their fishing in the sea, and about a mammoth whale that had been washed up on the shore. When Yamino-Kwiti asked him how they had caught the large fish, he told them about big wooden canoes the shore people made by lacing planks together with fiber and calking them with asphaltum, and that they fished from these canoes with spears, nets, and lines.

It was not till they were in their own huts for the night that Yamino-Kwiti found an opportunity to tell Mamish-Ahikañ about the kidnapping of the young Siba courier, Puku-Kakar, by their family enemies. "Hm-m," he said, "we shall have to have a council with Siba-vik when he comes."

The next morning Yamino-Kwiti and his playmates darted away to the south to the top of a big hill from which they could see the course of the Indian trail as it followed the riverbank to the sea.

"There they come!" shouted Tomear, and down the steep hill they raced, shouting and leaping, scaring the little rabbits into their holes among the brush, and rousing whole bevies of quail that flew with a great whirr of wings to a place more safe than the trail of whooping, excited Indian boys. Other animals of the wild, large and small, also retreated. Even Tukut, of the padded feet and the cat eyes, slunk into his den among the rocks and lay low, frightened by the great noise of the small boys.

"We'll run a race," shouted Wupu-Yatcho, "to see who gets there first." Wupu-Yatcho was always trying to convince himself that he, too, could someday run as fast as Yamino-Kwiti. Now he was too late, for Yamino-Kwiti was already in the lead with Tomear close at his heels, Wupu-Yatcho next, while in the rear came Puy-Puy, blowing and puffing, thrusting his head forward like the road runner for which he was named.

Such excitement when the boys reached the men! The women were bearing the heavily laden carrying nets on their backs and trailing along in the rear. Questions were asked, but no one heard the answers for the noise they made. As the party arrived at the pass between the two hills, all the men, women, and children of the village were there to meet them. Even the babies were there, nodding their little black heads over the shoulders of their mothers. Only the very old grandfathers and grandmothers were left in the village, because they were too old and feeble to take unnecessary steps.

When the party finally reached the village, the old folks were there, waiting, their wrinkled faces smiling and eager to hear all the party had to tell. Everyone wanted to see the things that had been brought from the shores of the sea and from the island peoples.

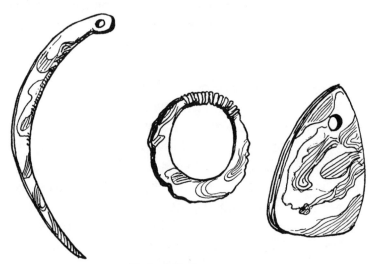

Abalone shell pendants.

There were seal and sea-otter skins, olivella, clam, and abalone shells, all very precious articles. Money would be made from the clam shells, and beads and rings from the abalone shells to adorn the necks and ears of both men and women. Fish-hooks would be made also from the abalone shells. There were beautiful, black pots of steatite, made only by the Indians on the island of Pimu, which were considered very precious. There would be busy times, now, for all the men and the women; even the children would do their parts to make good use of the things which the women were bringing in the carrying nets on their backs.

That night there was a great feast of fish and whale meat which smelled terribly, but the Indians did not mind, and they ate it with enjoyment while telling many stories around the fire. Ya-mino-Kwiti and the other boys sat on the ground in the outer circle to listen. Indian boys and girls were not allowed to gather too closely to the fire or to gaze into its fiery mystery for fear it would

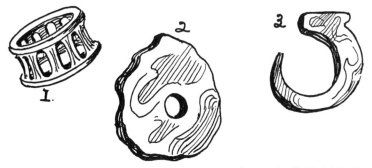

1. Fish vertebral finger ring.  2. Shell pendant.  3. Shell fishhook.

They saw Puku-Kakar tied to a tree.

"The moon! There is the moon!" he called again.

# 11

## The New Moon Races

"COME, COME, my boys! There is the new moon!" called old Wiku-am, as he stood with raised arm pointing to the western sky. Sure enough, there in the golden west was the very thin crescent of the new moon!

"The moon! There is the moon!" he called again. His voice, clear and strong, reached even the outermost huts of the village, and from every direction came the boys, large and small.

They did not have to be told what to do. That little crescent came regularly each month, and the Indian boys celebrated the event by running races. They did not know why they ran races at the appearance of the new moon, but even the oldest Indian could not remember a time when it had not been done. So the custom continued, and each new moon saw the boys racing in the afterglow.

Amid much laughing and pushing the big boys lined up, eager and ready for the signal to start.

"Get ready!" called Siba-vik. *"Pukú, wehé, páhe!* Go!" They were off!

Back at the starting point the small boys stood tense and excited, waiting for the big boys to reach the mark and return. Here they come!

Yamino-Kwiti holds his breath, for there in the lead is his uncle, Muka-Ayoin, the younger brother of his father. How that family can run! There! He has touched the goal far ahead of the others, and now Siba-vik is tying a new buckskin string around his neck. Muka-Ayoin has won that little mark of distinction almost every new moon for a long time. And each time Yamino-Kwiti's family pride swells again in his breast and makes him more determined than ever to be a courier that he may carry messages to the four corners of the earth. He hopes with all his ambitious little heart that his faithful practice at running will win for him his long-cherished desire.

Now it is the turn of the smaller boys. Yamino-Kwiti gives first place in the line to the chief's son, Tomear, while he takes second. His cousin, Puku-Kakar, comes next, and beside him is little Tcoar, whose fast legs cause Yamino-Kwiti much anxiety. Last in the line is Puy-Puy, who has run always like the road runner, with his head thrust forward, since he was a plump little bug catcher.

"Get ready!" calls Siba-vik, and he counts, "*Pukú, wehé, páhe!* Go!"

They needed no second urging. The five small boys ran with all their might. They could not be seen so easily now, for their small brown bodies merged into the fast-gathering shadows. Old Wikuam stood at the turning stone to touch each runner as he reached it, turned, and then ran back to the starting point where Siba-vik stood. All the village people were along the line, laughing, shouting, dancing up and down, and making so much noise that the thin little crescent of a moon must have been frightened, for it slipped down into the sea just as Yamino-Kwiti touched the goal ahead of Tcoar! He had won the buckskin string around his neck! Siba-vik patted him on the head and said, "You are like your father, Yamino-Kwiti, swift as a young antelope!"

Amid the distracting noise of the people enjoying themselves, running this way and that, and the men dancing in a circle and singing, Yamino-Kwiti sought his father.

"Father, Father!" he called. "See, I won the buckskin honor tonight! Siba-vik said I was like you, Father! Please ask Siba-vik if I may be a courier and not train for the *Yobagnar!*"

His father looked at him in astonishment. "Come, come, Yamino-Kwiti," he said, "do not be so excited. It is a great honor to be trained for the *Yobagnar*. You should be proud and not act so foolish."

"I'd rather run, Father, than dance and sing," said Yamino-Kwiti, in a calmer voice. "I'd rather see new places and learn new things than to stay in the *Yobagnar* and learn old legends and——"

"Yamino-Kwiti," his father interrupted sternly, "do not let anyone hear you say that again— not even the ears of the trees!"

"But, Father, you will speak to Siba-vik?"
asked Yamino-Kwiti, coming so close to his father
and looking up into his face in such a pleading
fashion that Mamish-Ahikañ spoke more gently,
saying, "Yes, Yamino-Kwiti, I shall speak."

Yamino-Kwiti, being no different from other
small boys, wanted to share his hopes with someone. He ran to tell Kihut-Kiur, who was the only
one of all the other children who sympathized with
him. The others were envious of the honor be-
stowed upon him which he despised.

As the twilight faded they could hear the old
men singing to the rhythm of their dance, one foot
then the other: *pom, pom-pom, pom, pom-pom*—
"As the moon dieth, and cometh to life again—"
*pom, pom-pom, pom, pom-pom*—"so we, also having to die, shall live again!"

"Shall live again," came the echo—*pom, pom-
pom, pom, pom-pom*—"live again!"

The next day his father told Yamino-Kwiti that
he had spoken to Siba-vik.

"What did he say, my father?" asked Yamino-
Kwiti, with hope strong in his voice.

"Yamino-Kwiti," his father said sternly, "you
are to be trained for the *Yobagnar.* If you are good
you will become a *Pul* in time, but first you will
be a *Púmal*—a young initiate."

Yamino-Kwiti gave his father one long look in
which all hope died, then he turned and slowly
left. He must not show his disappointment too

plainly; he was an Indian boy. He must take pain and pleasure as they came. He could laugh with joy, but he must never, never cry from pain or disappointment.

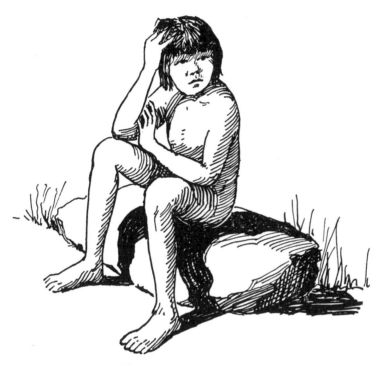

He must never, never cry.

# 12

# The Law of the Tribe

THE DAY after the new moon races, a messenger came running from Asuksa. Yamino-Kwiti and some of the other boys were squatting on their heels in the shade of an oak tree which stood close to the hut of Siba-vik. They were watching two of the men make money beads from the clam shells which had been brought from the seashore by the traders. When the messenger came up, panting and out of breath, they could not help hearing every word that he said.

"Asuksa-vik sends a message." He stopped long enough to draw a long breath. "His wife is dead. The medicine man got magic from your A-nub-su-voi-rot. Your courier was taken prisoner by three of our men. Thus the magic was captured and the cure delayed so that the patient died. The medicine man says the delay spoiled the magic. After the death ceremony Asuksa-vik will hold council with you."

Tomear went to stand by his father. The other boys were silent, waiting for the answer of Siba-vik. They were all concerned and involved in this affair, for the feud of the courier's family had led to trouble between the villagers themselves, which would have to be settled in conference.

"You will say to Asuksa-vik," answered Siba-vik, "that we shall hold council when he sends the word. The magic of A-nub-su-voi-rot is good magic. It is a great misfortune that the wife of your chief did not get it in time." He paused only a moment, then with the sharp intonation of the commander said, "Go!"

The messenger turned and, without waiting for anything further, took up his running stride. He was gone through the village, past the wondering villagers, and out of sight before they had time to thoroughly realize the import of his message: that the wife of Asuksa-vik was dead, and the three Indians from Asuksa who had waylaid Puku-Kakar were responsible!

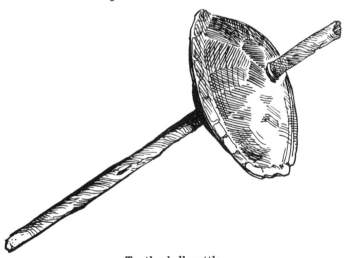

Turtle-shell rattle.

It was more than a week before the ceremony for the dead woman was completed and since the messenger from Asuksa had called Siba-vik and the Elders into council. Puku-Kakar, Tomear, Yamino-Kwiti, Wupu-Yatcho, and Puy-Puy went also. They were important witnesses since the offense had been directed at one of them, and the others had rescued both their own courier and the magic.

The official crier, Ya'iikat, had gone through the village, crying, "*O-a nahacua!*[33] Three men of Asuksa have been guilty of a crime. They are bad men! Come everyone! *O-a nahacua!*"*

When the people of both villages gathered at Asuksa, all the old men from both lodges sat in a circle, Siba-vik and Asuksa-vik sitting opposite each other in the center. The prisoners sat to one side, and the witnesses to the other, of the two chiefs. The whole village of Asuksa and many people from Siba gathered about the outer edge of the circle. Yamino-Kwiti thought he would never forget that conference. The members of both feuding families sat and glared at each other. When Indians hate they hate long and hard, and these two families had hated one another for many generations—for so long that no one now living could remember what had started the quarrel.

Asuksa-vik was a kindly but stern man. He was hardly recognizable as he sat bowed and grave,

* O-ah na-ha-koo'-a.

with all his thick black hair cut off and his mourning mask[34] dried upon his face. His was the great
loss in this affair, since his wife had died, although
the offense had been enacted by three of his men
against one of their own enemies. That this enemy
happened to be a courier hurrying on business
from a medicine man of one village to one of another made the offense more serious. It was a
question of the laws and government of the villages
themselves as well as one of their deep and abiding
reverence for the business of their medicine men.

For hours the group deliberated. Questions were
asked and answered. The medicine men were not
questioned as to the nature of the packet which had
been stolen, for their secrets and knowledge were
sacred to their profession. Instead, their advice
was requested.

All five of the boys had to tell their part in the
affair. Two of the three offenders were brothers
and the third a cousin, making all three of them
members of the family which was the ancient enemy of the courier's ancestors.

The council was not to consider the family feud.
It was to deal with the interference of a courier
and the fact that such interference caused the
death of the wife of the chief. Because family
dissension was the cause of the attack on the person of Puku-Kakar, it was discussed, but dismissed
in view of the greater crime.

There was no question of their guilt—it was the

nature of their punishment that needed delibera-
tion and decision. There was no form of whipping
used among them. They paid for their mistakes
by either goods or money beads, and if the mistake
were considered a crime, such as murder, or trick-
ery against the lodge itself, there was only one
other form of punishment to be considered—death
by arrow shooting.

It was only recently that two of these culprits
had been forced to pay a whole *sayako*[19] to Koti-
Cuit for the burning of his house and possessions,
a burning which ended eventually in the death of
the grandmother in the hut. Now they had nothing
with which to pay a fine should the council consider
such punishment sufficient. Everyone was solemn
when finally the death sentence was passed upon
the three guilty kidnappers, and the execution was
carried out almost immediately.

The Indian law had been upheld and the sanctity
of both courier and medicine man vindicated. The
bodies of the three culprits were given to their
families to be disposed of. The disgrace of the
manner of their death went deeper in their Indian
souls than the grief over their loss.

Yamino-Kwiti and Puku-Kakar were filled with
awe and respect for the Indian laws and were two
solemn boys as they walked back over the trail to
Siba. They knew that never again would the boy
with the crooked toe annoy them with his tricks.

They were watching two men make money beads when a messenger
came from Asuksa.

Yamino-Kwiti found himself singing and stamping in time with the others.

But they did not forget that there were other members of that enemy family, and that now each one of them would have more fuel to add to his fire of hatred.

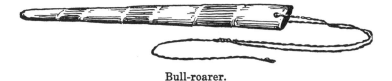

Bull-roarer.

# 13

# The Song Fight

HEN THE VILLAGERS of Siba returned to their village the grandfather of Yamino-Kwiti, the oldest member of the family, called a family gathering.

"We must have our song fight now," he said, "to prevent their curses from injuring us. We shall make it strong and long so that they can have no power whatever, and their line will die out."

Puku-Kakar and Muka-Ayoin were sent to neighboring hamlets to call together all members of their famliy, even to the very distant cousins.

For several days small and large groups came hurrying to Siba. They came from Akura, Yan,[8] Wenot, Shua, Sisitkano, Kukomo, Pieakhehe, Hutuk, and even Asuksa.

Among the ancestors of Yamino-Kwiti were many swift runners, or couriers, who from the very nature of their vocations saw more of the other people of the world than the more lazy stay-at-home members of the village. Therefore there had been more marriages in far, out-of-the-way places, and cousins and more cousins came into Siba at the bidding of the couriers.

There would be an abundance of food needed for this large gathering. The women and girls of the family at Siba gathered wood for fires and seeds and berries from the fields. The men hunted and brought in antelope, deer, mountain sheep, and other game. The small children hunted insects. They had learned very early—from the time they could toddle—to catch something to eat, and bugs such as grasshoppers and fat grubs were the first things. Then came small, slippery snakes, blinking lizards, field mice, and many other denizens of the small-animal world. The children were then considered able to provide for themselves to some extent. The boys caught squirrels, rats, rabbits—both jack rabbits and cottontails—quail, and partridges from the fields, wild ducks from the marsh, and fish from the river.

Although the rest of the village had no enmity with the family at Asuksa, the recent crime and execution had involved the whole village and gave the song fight added interest and importance to all of them. Many joined in the feast and sang and danced their hate in unison with the family of the couriers.

Even after the feast had begun there were more cousins from distant places hurrying to Siba to add force and numbers to the family song fight.

For eight days and nights the feast and dances continued. As they danced they sang and stamped their feet. The songs were not the kind to cheer

and soften the heart, but rather were terrible
songs of hate and curses.

Many made up the words of their own songs,
and as they repeated them over and over, others
took up the refrain, which added to the volume,
rhythm, and emphasis.

Yamino-Kwiti found himself singing and
stamping his feet in time with the others. He sang
at the top of his lungs:

> Tamít shall wither their berries,
> Tamít shall scorch their bodies;
> Moar shall show them to their enemies;
> The Shu-shyot[35] shall forget them;
> Ahikañ shall blow away their seeds;
> And Wenot shall flood their homes!

They stopped only to eat, and while eating,
rested. Sometimes Puku-Kakar and Yamino-
Kwiti found themselves together in the midst of
the other members of their family, thumping and
stamping and repeating their songs over and over
with diabolical cadence.

> From our feet comes Tauwaro on their graves—
> They have no rest in Tucupar.
> Our curses follow them into the underworld,
> And Taquich strikes them down!

The villagers who watched from the outskirts
of this dancing, whirling, and singing mob could
feel the earth shake as the hundreds of feet
stamped, thumped, and beat out their rhythm.
Thump, thumpity thump! Stamp, stamp! Thump,

thumpity thump! Through their feet they brought Tauwaro, the thunder, upon the earth, and all felt sure that their enemies in the underworld and those yet to go there would feel it and be troubled.

By the eighth day their strength began to flag. They had used all the hateful words in their language and had used them over and over again. No new words could be found. As their vigor began to wane, their curses lost their force. Their efforts to disturb the sleep of their enemies by stamping on their graves lessened and died of sheer weariness. One by one they dropped out to crawl into their wickiups to sleep. Finally the whole family slept, some where they dropped on the ground in their exhaustion. All night, all day, they slept. And the song fight was over.

Yamino-Kwiti slept.

# 14

# Yamino-Kwiti Turns Eavesdropper

N THE OCTOBER moon, when the dry winds whistle across the valley from north and east, the people of Siba prepared to leave the village for the mountains. Each autumn they went to gather their annual harvest of large acorns from the mountain oaks and the sweet nuts from the piñon trees. Everywhere the grass was brown and sear, and the leaves of the sycamore were already yellow. The journey to the mountains must be made before the winter storms began, for then the mountains would be cold and sometimes white with snow.

It was a long line of villagers with their baskets and carrying nets that went along the river trail toward the mountains. The men went first; then came the women, some with babies on their backs, some with carrying nets full of provisions and utensils; lastly came the children, running and calling here and there. It took them nearly two days to go to their harvesting place, which no other Indian tribe was allowed to use. Nor were they expected to invade any other section, no matter how enticing the harvest might seem. Year after year each tribe and each village went to the same place to gather acorns and piñon nuts. The gathering was done by the women and children while the men hunted. The same spreading trees or caves were used each year for storage, the same great rocks used by the same tribes until the shallow little hollows where they ground the acorn meal were worn down into the hard rock as deep as bowls.

On the trail Kihut-Kiur carried her baby brother on her back, for her mother was already burdened with a large carrying net full of provisions. She wore a little basket cap to protect her forehead from the heavy, straining band of the net. The little girl watched with wistful eyes as the boys ran here and there along the trail, each with his throwing stick, sling, or arrows, making short excursions into the brush to do their youthful hunting. More than one surprised rabbit fell as they threw their sticks, and some of the boys were quick enough to catch quail.

Kihut-Kiur could not see Yamino-Kwiti anywhere and was glad when Manisar,[10] Tomear's sister, walked with her and carried Anusetaxai, the baby, some of the way. She chirped to him like a little bird to make him smile, turning her head until she could feel his soft little cheek against her own, while the little fellow gurgled and crowed with delight.

Tomear walked with them for a moment. "Have you seen Yamino-Kwiti?" he asked.

No one had seen him since they left the camping place that morning, before Tamít, the sun, had risen above the mountains, and who was shining now some little distance above their tops. Where could Yamino-Kwiti be?

Perhaps, someone suggested, he had gone ahead with the men, so Tomear bounded away up the trail to find Yamino-Kwiti.

"Oh, Tomear! Come back!" called Manisar. "Look over there! Shukat! Look!"

Tomear stopped and looked where Manisar was pointing. Not far away Shukat, the deer, was capering in a very strange manner in the brush, showing his head and horns, and then disappearing completely, only to rear up as though standing on hind legs and prancing.

"That's a queer way for Shukat to act," said Tomear. "I wonder what's the matter with him. I'm going to see."

"Oh, don't, Tomear!" said his sister. "Maybe Tukut, the panther, or Icauvut, the wolf, are hunting him!"

But Tomear had fitted his arrow into his bow and was already stealing through the brush toward the place where he had last seen Shukat. The women, unaware of the children's affairs, went stolidly along the trail, heads bent to their burdens and feet planted firmly and persistently as they walked along the trail already made plain by the feet of the men.

Tomear crept silently toward Shukat, who had ceased to caper. Something was moving in the brush just ahead, and Tomear braced himself with his bow drawn and arrow ready. And then a strange thing happened! Tomear could hardly believe his eyes. On one side of the purple sagebrush just ahead of him he could see the bare foot of an Indian boy, and before he could say *"Nio mare!"* —"bless me!"—there was Shukat's head thrusting itself toward him around the other side of the bush. He looked so strange—so dried up and old— that Tomear did not draw his bow but stood still, wondering.

"Why don't you shoot me?" said Shukat, and Tomear, who never before had heard a human voice come from an animal, turned and ran. He had heard all his life the legends related by the elders in which the animals conversed with men, but this was the first time it had ever happened to him. He could hear Shukat running after him, and his heart pounded with terror, lending wings to his feet.

Suddenly he became aware that Manisar and Kihut-Kiur were standing on the trail, giggling and squealing with laughter. That brought him to his senses quickly. He couldn't let the girls laugh at him, so he turned to face the talking and running Shukat. There was Yamino-Kwiti, laughing so hard he could hardly hold the false deer head on his shoulders. The children were convulsed with merriment. Some of the women, hearing the laughter, turned and laughed with them, adding to Tomear's chagrin.

"Where did you get that deer head?" asked Kihut-Kiur of Yamino-Kwiti.

"Someone dropped it off his pack, and I found it," he answered and went into a perfect gale of laughter again. Tomear could not laugh. He had been too thoroughly frightened to recover so quickly. Besides, his pride had been hurt, and he turned and walked up the trail, leaving the other three still convulsed with mirth.

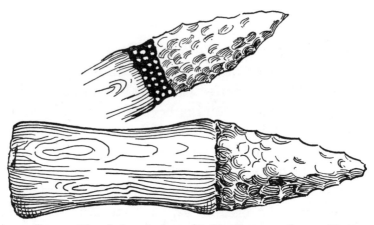

Stone cutting knives had wooden handles, sometimes with mother-of-pearl inlay set in asphalt.

By the time the women and children had reached the camping ground the men were already there. They had killed several deer and antelope and were waiting about, some of them stretched out in the sunshine on the bare rocks, some cutting poles for their shelters, until the women would come to make the fires and cook the meat.

The women were glad to lay down their burdens and hustle about for firewood. After the hungry people had been fed the matter of shelter for the night had to be thought of. In the mountains the nights were colder. Besides, there were large animals in the mountains. Not only huge Hunar, but others even more dangerous, as Tukut, the panther, Icauvut of the wolf pack, and other night prowlers whose eyes could see what no man's could see in the dark.

When the villagers had left Siba, Mamish-Ahikañ had not returned from a run to Kukumo, but he appeared in camp to report to Siba-vik just as the last ray of sunlight disappeared from the tips of the mountains. He was tired and very hungry, and Yamino-Kwiti's mother hastened to prepare his food.

Yamino-Kwiti had helped with the making of their shelter, and, in the absence of Mamish-Ahikañ, his uncle, Muka-Ayoin, had cut the poles and brush to fashion their abode. It was ready now, and Yamino-Kwiti's mother was busy arranging their belongings. Yamino-Kwiti took advantage of her occupation to slip away on noiseless bare feet toward the campfire where Siba-vik and the Council of Elders sat in a circle to hear the report of Mamish-Ahikañ.

Yamino-Kwiti knew that he should not be there,

but as the shadows hid him completely, he allowed
his curiosity to get the better of him. The interesting tales his father usually told about the country into which he went and which the other Indians
did not see always held him spellbound. They fired
his imagination, and his desire to see these strange
places was fast becoming an obsession with him.

Each day that he had to sit with Pul Maat in
the village and repeat over and over what was said
to him, he had rebelled more and more. It had become harder and harder to keep Pul Maat from
seeing his rebelliousness. The things he had to
repeat were tales of long ago, legends of tiresome
length about his long-dead forefathers, and the
words of songs to be sung at ceremonies. Yamino-
Kwiti had questioned Pul Maat about those things
which he desired most to know; what was on the
other side of the mountains and where did the sea
end; all those things about the great world outside
his own valley. Pul Maat had been silent and had
looked at Yamino-Kwiti with such reproach in his
small black eyes and somber face that for some
reason Yamino-Kwiti had felt ashamed. Finally,
he ceased to question the old man and buried his
great desire in his own heart as well as he could.

Where there is desire there is some action toward
its fulfillment. Yamino-Kwiti's desire had taken
him, all too often, into situations where he had to
remind himself that small Indian boys were not
allowed to interfere—nor to listen when the elders

Tomear had fitted his arrow into his bow.

"I must go myself," he answered.

talked the business of the tribe. Twice this summer, however, he had been active in the affairs of the village, and this notoriety had broken down some of his childish reticence with his elders. He felt almost grown up and mature enough to share his father's news. So he stood still in the dark and listened.

The men about the fire talked in low tones, and the smoke from their long, thin pipes mingled with the smoke of the fire. Now and then a few excited words could be distinguished above the low murmur. "Mu-ku-pia-bet. . . . Ma-yain-ta-lap.[36] . . . Many men killed! . . . Women and children captives. . . ." were some of the words he heard until an unknown fear held him rooted to the spot, and cold chills went up and down his bare brown body.

Then he heard his mother calling, "Yamino-Kwiti! Where are you?" He did not answer, so close to the campfire had he strayed. They must not know that he had been where no Indian boy should be—listening in on his elders—so with swift feet he bounded over the pine needles to his mother before he answered her.

"Here I am, my mother," he said. Suddenly the strange fear left him, and, throwing his arms about his mother, he buried his face in the fur of the cape she wore and vowed silently he would never let the Ma-yain-ta-lap or any other cruel tribe take his mother captive. He would be a warrior, as well as a courier, in spite of Pul Maat!

"Are you cold that you shiver, Yamino-Kwiti?" his mother asked. He took the rabbitskin blanket she gave him but did not mention the cause of his trembling. He crawled into his shelter, but it was not until both his mother and his father were sound asleep that Yamino-Kwiti's excited brain gave way to slumber. Of all the village folk only the watchers at the fire were awake. They did not dare sleep, for in the circle of deep dark around the camp could be seen the shining jewels that were the eyes of Tukut, the panther, or those of Icauvut and his pack. Wushi and the other dogs in the camp lay with bristling coats and low growls in their throats, but the tired village folk slept soundly.

A multitude of little bright-eyed creatures, clad in somber brown and gray, came out of hiding and scampered about on agile feet, communing with their own, evading their enemies, and becoming hunters of food. On silent wings bats and owls glided through the trees and pounced on the unwary little creatures.

In the night the wind changed its direction. The *nanah*, or ears of the trees, had heard many things this day. Now there was whispering among all the night people of the forest. The wind had picked up the various scents and smells of an Indian camp and carried them with the fragrance of pine and wood smoke through the trees and along the watercourses.

The drowsy watchers at the fire were roused by

soft thuds near by among the piñon trees. "We
shall find piñon cones on the ground when it is
morning," they said to one another. Little did they
know that the sensitive nose of Hunar had picked
the smell of men from the wind. She had roused
from her sleep and, stretching to her full height,
had sharpened her long, knifelike claws on the
rough bark of a piñon tree, leaving her marks
eight feet above the ground. Pine cones ready to
drop had thudded to the ground, but Hunar did
not bother with them. As silently as her huge body
would permit, she ambled off until the scent of
man no longer disturbed her.

Stones used to grind acorn meal.

# 15

# Yamino-Kwiti Takes Things into His Own Hands

ONG BEFORE Tamít, the sun, poked his shining face above the rim of the mountains in the east the Indians were busy. Their day started with the usual bath in the river. Without exception they found the water colder than the river that flowed past Siba. There was much splashing and squealing and jumping up and down as they came out of the cold water and ran to the fire to dry and warm themselves. The women laughed at the children and made fun of them for shivering, and the children tried their best to stop the chattering of their teeth. They succeeded only after vigorous exercise that caused their naked brown bodies to glow with life and vitality. Their bright, black eyes glistened, and their childish cheeks were red with health. The blue tattoo marks[37] on the faces of the girls and women showed more plainly than ever, and their mothers looked at them with fond admiration. When they were small girls they wore no other thing in the way of adornment or covering, and these marks were put there to enhance their beauty.

They ate their cold acorn-meal mush and rabbit stew with infinite enjoyment and were ready for the day's work—work which was full of delight and anticipation for it meant food for the rest of the winter. The chief purpose of an Indian's life was to gather food which nature supplied him, and he was caused no further labor than that of gathering and preparing it. Besides, the greater part of the work was done by the women, who accepted it as a privilege.

Water bottle-basket, and others full of acorns and acorn meal.

They got out the baskets, and the children scampered to the oak trees to gather the acorns. Gray squirrels waved their graceful plumed tails and, chattering at the invaders, fled to safer haunts. It was well that they did, for the trees were soon full of Indian children shaking the limbs and picking the acorns, which they dropped into baskets below. They would catch some of those squirrels later, for beautiful plumed squirrels make good Indian food, and squirrel fur is as warm in an Indian blanket as it is on the squirrel's back.

While the women and children were gathering acorns and leaching the meal,[38] there were others gathering the nuts from the piñon trees. These were harder to get, for the cones grew high in the trees and had to be picked off. If shaken down, the delicious little nuts would fall out of the cones and be lost among the pine needles on the ground. The unopened cones were heated in order to extract the nuts. They did not have to be cracked and leached as the acorns did, for they were sweet and delicious just as they grew and could be cracked by their teeth.

The baskets of nuts and acorn meal were given to the care of Siba-vik, since the nut gathering was a community affair, and the work was done by all who were able to do it.

Yamino-Kwiti and Kihut-Kiur had worked together the better part of the first morning, and Yamino-Kwiti could not help confiding to her the snatches of talk he had heard at the campfire the evening before.

"Oh, Yamino-Kwiti, do you think the Ma-yain-ta-lap will go to Siba?" she asked, with her eyes wide with terror.

"I don't know, Kihut-Kiur," he answered, stopping in his work of shaking down the acorns to wonder himself if, when they returned, they would see their village in ruins and those old ones who had remained, slaughtered or taken prisoners. Suddenly he started: "Listen, Kihut-Kiur! Someone must go and tell them to hide—or—or they may be killed!"

"But, Yamino-Kwiti, if you ask someone to go they will know you listened at the council fire!"

"Then, Kihut-Kiur, I must go myself!" he answered, as he scrambled down from the limb on which he had been sitting. The two children looked at each other. He was pretty young to travel alone in the mountains, and each child was aware of the dangers he would meet on the trail. It did not occur to either of them that this matter of safety for their village would be attended to by the elders and Siba-vik.

"Perhaps they will not miss me if I go at once," Yamino-Kwiti said. "You must not tell them that I have gone."

"Of course not!" answered the little girl. She knew she would have to work that much harder with Yamino-Kwiti gone, for she would have to shake the tree as well as pick up the acorns from the ground. "They will know when I bring in the baskets alone."

"If they ask you where I am, tell them you do not know. And I will go as fast as I can, and be back—real soon," he said, not knowing just how fast he could go for so long a distance. "I'll run all the way."

"I will not be *yayare*," she said. "I'll just keep silent."

He knew that his father, the courier, went on his long runs without provisions or weapons of any sort, trusting his speed to carry him safely on his errand. This was the only time Indians ever traveled alone, for they usually hunted in pairs or groups for safety's sake and always had weapons. Without even a good-by to the little girl, he started on his self-imposed mission just as he was—as naked as the wind.

Down the trail he bounded. This was the easiest part of his journey for it was all downhill. He almost bumped into a flock of bighorn sheep, and his sudden entry into their midst sent them scurrying in all directions. The old ram, however, stood his ground firmly in the middle of the trail, and Yamino-Kwiti had to stop. The ram charged with lowered horns, but Yamino-Kwiti dodged so nimbly that the animal almost went over the edge of the trail into the canyon below. Yamino-Kwiti instantly took advantage of the time it took the ram to retrieve his balance and bounded past him. On he went like the wind, tearing down the slopes, around boulders, and over rough places. He did not look behind to see whether the ram was following or not, or whether he had rejoined his ewes after dutifully protecting them from the danger of an Indian boy.

It was fast getting dark when he came to the outskirts of Siba. He noticed that there was no smoke coming out of the huts, no barking dogs. A sudden terror came into his heart. Had the Ma-yain-ta-lap, the big-bow men, already been there? He must be cautious, now, and approach without being seen. Softly he slipped into the shadows of the willows and cottonwoods along the stream and followed them to the edge of the village. He could hear no sound. Quietly he passed from hut to hut. Not a soul was there!

What had happened? He saw no signs of violence. Surely there had been a thorough exodus, for even their provisions and utensils were gone. All was as quiet as the desert when the moon is dark.

Where had his people gone? Then he remembered the hiding place which had never been used during his short lifetime but which all his people knew and had used in years gone by—the caves and narrow pass at a canyon's mouth into the mountains. He would go there and see.

Suddenly, he realized he was very tired but did not dare lie down to sleep in the deserted village. The emptiness of it filled him with apprehension, and every sound of the night might mean enemies —the big-bow men, the Ma-yain-ta-lap!

He sat on a boulder under the drooping boughs

of a willow tree and got his breath. He laid his head on his arms which were folded across his up-drawn knees. For just a moment he dozed but was roused suddenly by the realization that some-one, or something, was very close to him. A dark form emerged from the bushes, and a cold nose thrust itself into his face.

"Ni-Wushi!" he exclaimed. "You followed me!" And he threw his arms around the neck of his dog. He was no longer alone nor unprotected.

Together the boy and his dog made their way in the dark along the trail to the north through the tall grass and around the miry ground where the tules grew. This would take him a good part of the night and would delay his return, but it must be done. He was too tired to run, and, be-sides, the immediate danger which had urged him on and lent wings to his feet was over; but he must find out if his people were safe.

The gray light which precedes the dawn was spreading over the sky when Yamino-Kwiti and Wushi came to the mouth of the canyon. Over the tops of the chaparral he could see a dark head bobbing up and down as someone ran along the trail. Quickly Yamino-Kwiti withdrew into the bushes at his side, drawing Wushi with him. He would wait and let the Indian runner pass, who-ever he might be.

So lightly did the runner advance that they could not hear his footsteps until he passed them, running as swiftly as the wind. Yamino-Kwiti jumped to his feet. There was only one runner who ran like that! Mamish-Ahikañ!

"Father! My father!" called Yamino-Kwiti, as he started after the courier.

"*Nio mare!* Yamino-Kwiti, is that you?"

"Yes, it is I," and Yamino-Kwiti felt very sheepish in spite of his brave purpose, for he knew he had been guilty of something no Indian boy should do—listening to the elders and taking upon himself a mission such as his.

"Yamino-Kwiti, why are you here?"

"I came to warn our people of the Ma-yain-ta-lap!"

For a moment Mamish-Ahikañ looked at his son. "And how did you know about the Ma-yain-ta-lap?" he asked finally.

"I heard you tell Siba-vik that they had killed all the people at Mu-ku-pia-bet and had come down the valley of Wachbit[8] and that you had feared they might cross the valley west of Toibi[8]——"
He paused at the unusual expression of severity on his father's face.

"Is that all you heard?" the courier's voice was stern.

"Yes, that is all I heard."

"Did you not know that Siba-vik would not let our people be unwarned? That it is his business—not a child's—to protect his people?"

"My father, I did not think—I did not think

anything but that Grandfather and all the others might be killed by the Ma-yain-ta-lap."

"Yamino-Kwiti, your heart is good, but your head is young. You have affection, I am sure, but you must also have wisdom, which comes with many suns. After this you must wait for your commands."

"Yes, Father," said Yamino-Kwiti, and he felt very, very tired.

"I cannot stay and talk with you, Yamino-Kwiti, but you must rest only a little while and then go back as quickly as you can. Pul Maat will talk with you, tomorrow." He turned and left Yamino-Kwiti standing in the middle of the trail with the tall grass growing on either side—a tired and crestfallen little Indian boy.

He would have liked to follow his father, but he knew that fast as he could run, he could not keep up with that fleet messenger, Mamish-Ahikañ. Besides, he had been traveling all night, and now that there was no longer need for hurry, he lay down and slept.

So soundly did he sleep he did not hear Wushi growl, but he awoke with a start when Wushi licked his face and whined.

"What is it, Ni-Wushi?" he asked, and he knew by the dog's actions that someone was approaching. Then he heard the soft thud, thud, thud of feet on the trail, and, peering through the bushes, he saw another runner going in the opposite direction from that taken by Mamish-Ahikañ. It was the runner from Asuksa.

"*Ycuaro!*[39] Here!" called Yamino-Kwiti.

The courier turned and came back to Yamino-Kwiti. "Who are you?" he asked.

"I am Yamino-Kwiti, son of Mamish-Ahikañ of Siba," he answered. "I came to warn our people of the Ma-yain-ta-lap." Yamino-Kwiti enjoyed the startled expression on the face of the runner.

"The Ma-yain-ta-lap? But you came from the west! The Ma-yain-ta-lap were in the east!"

"We—my father and I—went to warn our people, and I am now returning to the mountains."

"I see. And what do you know of the Ma-yain-ta-lap?"

"I know they came down through Wachbit and killed the people of Mu-ku-pia-bet on the way, robbed and burned the towns as they came, and then camped near Toibi."

"Toibi?" exclaimed the courier. "Camped near Toibi? Then you did not know that the Ma-yain-ta-lap have left Toibi? They are returning to Tahachapi[8] in the north, from where they came."

"You are certain?" asked Yamino-Kwiti, unable to believe that his fears had no longer any reason for existing.

"Surely. I just came from Toibi. There is no one left, and the houses are burned," answered the runner from Asuksa. "*Yamu uimi*, I am going."

*"Mea,* go!" answered Yamino-Kwiti. He stood
with his hand on his dog's neck and watched the
runner from Asuksa until the chaparral hid him
from sight.

The way back to the mountains seemed much,
much farther to Yamino-Kwiti. There was no
longer the thought of danger to spur him on, and
now the way was all uphill.

It was midafternoon when he reached the foot
of the mountain trail and met Koti-Cuit hurrying
toward him.

"I came to find you," said his uncle. "You were
so slow getting here."

Slow? Yamino-Kwiti slow? And he had prided
himself on being swift of foot! Somehow this business of trying to be a courier in spite of everything
and against the dominance of Pul Maat was not so
full of glory and good results as he had hoped it
might be. It seemed to be continually making
trouble for him.

"There is no need to hurry any more," he said.

"With enemies on the warpath?" asked his
uncle.

"But the Ma-yain-ta-lap have gone back to
Tahachapi from where they came."

"How do you know that, Yamino-Kwiti?" asked
his uncle.

"I met the runner from Asuksa who said he had
just come from Toibi and that the Ma-yain-ta-lap
had gone back the way they came."

"That is good news!" said Koti-Cuit. "Come, we shall tell Siba-vik."

As he went up the trail behind his uncle, Yamino-Kwiti regained his feeling of importance. Had he not brought news to his people as a courier should?

In his elation he picked up the shining brown horse chestnuts where the trail led under the buckeye trees and shied them at the blue jays. They chattered maliciously above his head in the autumn foliage of the trees.

He lost some of his feeling of importance, however, as soon as he stood in front of Pul Maat and listened to the deep, bearlike voice of the old man who scolded and told him he must forget his idea of being a courier, for he was to be a *Púmal* very soon now. He marched Yamino-Kwiti off for another period of instruction in which he had to repeat words that he did not know. The meaning of them would be taught later, but now both his ear and his memory were being put to the test. Pul Maat did not know that soon Yamino-Kwiti was to put this training to good use.

A day or so later, when the day's harvesting of nuts and acorns had been done and the evening feast was being prepared, Muka-Ayoin, Puku-Kakar, and Yamino-Kwiti took their bows and arrows and hastened up the watercourse. They had seen in the wet sand by the creek the tracks of the soft-padded one, Tukut, the panther. The tracks led them along the sandy bank over the slope toward the territory of Asuksa-vik's nut gathering. They went quickly for they had little daylight left in which to hunt the wild beast.

Coming to the edge of the arroyo, Muka-Ayoin stooped to examine the prints of Tukut's padded feet and stopped suddenly, motioning to the two boys just behind him to be silent. A few feet below him on a terrace above the creekbed was Tukut, crouched and ready to spring! Looking to see what Tukut had selected as a victim, Muka-Ayoin started and hastily fitted an arrow to his large, strong bow.

Peering through the bushes the two boys saw an Indian girl standing on the opposite side of the little stream. She had a large water basket on her head. Here eyes were wide with fright, and she seemed unable to move!

Swish! went the arrow from Muka-Ayoin's bow. Just in time it struck Tukut at the base of his skull, severing the spinal cord. Two more arrows followed in such quick succession that Tukut had time only for the impulse of his spring, which, being checked so unexpectedly from the rear, caused him to fall almost at the feet of the Indian girl. She gave a little cry, dropped her water basket, and bounded up the slope, her grass skirt catching in the bushes as she fled.

"Don't go!" called Muka-Ayoin. "Tukut is dead!"

She stopped her mad flight and came back down

the slope, pushing the bushes to one side as she came. "Who are you?" she asked in the language which they all knew.

"I am Muka-Ayoin from Siba. And you?"

"I am Kicha-Shungal from Asuksa, but my mother comes from Pala."[8] She pointed to the body of Tukut. "You came just in time, Muka-Ayoin, and your name is good." Catching up her water basket, she vanished up the bank among the underbrush.

Muka-Ayoin watched her go, then turning to the boys, said, "She is *cabatcho*—good-looking. Come, help me skin Tukut. The light will be gone soon."

It was quite dark when they found their way back to camp with the skin and carcass of Tukut.

The two younger boys quickly forgot Kicha-Shungal, but Muka-Ayoin remembered her so well that, when the nut harvest was over and they were all back in the village, he and his brothers sent gifts to her people in Asuksa so that they might arrange for her marriage to Muka-Ayoin.

Tukut.

# 16

## Muk-Ayoin Becomes a Warrior

OW CAME the time when the big winds whistled through the trees with a cold breath, and the villagers were all busy making their huts waterproof with new tule thatch. When they had returned from the mountains, their baskets were so full of piñon nuts, acorns, and acorn meal that they had to set to work at once to build new huts to shelter their harvest before the winter rains began. Besides, there was an unusual number of large, heavy skins of mountain animals packed in rolls, and all these things, including the bright-colored feathers of the mountain birds, must be put under cover.

The *chamucas*, or large storage baskets, were filled to capacity with the harvest, so the old women made more of them out of willow withes and tule rushes, and their old fingers worked diligently to complete them.

The men cut willow poles for new huts, set them in the ground, and tied them together in a round, domelike framework. The women gathered tule rushes from the marshes to cover them, and the children helped in the work. Even the little girls carried loads of tules like little pack animals. Yamino-Kwiti worked as hard as he could, hoping thus to evade Pul Maat and the tedious hours of training. But Pul Maat was busy himself. He was repairing the *Yoba*.

When Yamino-Kwiti saw what Pul Maat was doing he wondered if he were getting the *Yoba* ready for the ceremony in which Yamino-Kwiti would be made a *Púmal*. Yamino-Kwiti's face assumed the stubborn look which meant real Indian resistance. He began to think up ways and means to avoid it. But Yamino-Kwiti was mistaken. It was another ceremony for which Pul Maat was preparing.

While the women had been working on the *chamucas* and the new huts, the men had gathered behind the windbreaks about their wickiups. They basked in the warm sunshine where they could not feel the wind. They talked and laughed as people do when they rest, but their recent fright, caused by enemies as near to them as Toibi, turned their talk to war, weapons, and warriors. They talked of the poison which the medicine men made for their spearheads and of its quickness in working. And they bragged considerably.

Behind the windbreak of the hut of Siba-vik was another group of men. They talked of warriors, also, and Pul Maat had joined them. They were naming over the youths of the village who were old enough to be initiated into the warrior class. It was the warrior ceremony for which Pul

Maat and some of the elders had been repairing the *Yoba*.

Yamino-Kwiti and his comrades were not yet old enough to be among those named, but his young uncle, Muka-Ayoin, was. He was older than Yamino-Kwiti, but much younger than his two brothers, Koti-Cuit and Mamish-Ahikañ.

If any of the youths selected for warriors had fears or dislikes of the ceremonies they were to undergo, they did not show it, for then even the women would scorn them. No Indian, even of this good-natured tribe of which the people of Siba were a part, ever allowed himself to show fear of pain. It was endured with as great an indifference as was possible.

Their philosophy of life taught them to endure suffering and privation without protest, but it did not take into consideration the difference between necessary and unnecessary suffering. They felt that if a person could endure pain from inflicted torture he was a brave man and could face life without fear. So they were cruel to one another and themselves in their ceremonies. Such was their custom, and it never occurred to Muka-Ayoin to rebel. He knew what he had to endure and faced it with a grim determination to laugh through its duration.

It was bad enough, he knew, to be beaten with stinging nettles until it was impossible to move, but the most disagreeable part of the warrior cere-

mony was the big red-ant hill. Every Indian youth
did his best to make the others think it was pleasant. Each knew in his heart what torture it was
to be laid on an anthill and have the infuriated
ants crawl over his naked body, into eyes, ears,
nose, and mouth, biting and stinging until the pain
was almost unendurable. But each Indian went
through it, even to his gathering up handfuls of
the insects as a last act of bravado and swallowing
them alive. Noisy approval always met this daring
act each time an initiate warrior performed it, but
he never realized his actions were more like those
of a foolish child than of a really brave man who
faces real trouble as it comes.

Yamino-Kwiti, being younger, did not feel like
a warrior. He did not like to think of his uncle
Muka-Ayoin being subjected to suffering in any
way. Already he was rebelling against the thought
of his own freedom being taken from him by having to train for the *Yobagnar*, and this seed of rebelliousness included the warrior ceremony also.
Unfamiliar, grim lines showed on his little round
face. But his uncle had no such feelings. Though
he did his part as bravely as any of them, he had
not been able to laugh all through it. To him it
was a necessary evil.

Each youth was now supposed to be able to stand
almost any feat of endurance without protest.
They were entitled to the larger weapons of the
warriors, to the feathered headdress and war

paint, and were instructed in the art of war, of torture, and scalping.

It was not often that these good-natured people went to war, but when they did they ceased to be good-natured and were exceedingly cruel, torturing and then killing their prisoners with a fierce ruthlessness.

Some of the older men, who had weathered more than one war, had among their treasures many scalps of their enemies which were exhibited with pride whenever the talk turned to war and deeds of daring.

When the ceremony had ended the young warriors went to their huts to sleep, for they were exhausted. Yamino-Kwiti followed Muka-Ayoin into the wickiup where the recently initiated warrior threw himself on the ground and buried his face in his arms. Yamino-Kwiti came and sat beside him, unable to express the sympathy he felt, not realizing that sympathy was the last thing Muka-Ayoin wanted. He was now of the warrior class and above sympathy!

Finally Yamino-Kwiti spoke. "Muka-Ayoin."

At the sound of a voice, Muka-Ayoin sat up suddenly. He looked at Yamino-Kwiti wildly with bloodshot eyes and swollen face.

"What do you want?" he demanded. "What are you doing here?"

"When I am grown up," said Yamino-Kwiti in a boyish effort to comfort someone who didn't want comforting, "if they make a *Pul* of me, I am not going to let them have a warrior ceremony!"

"What!" exclaimed Muka-Ayoin. "No warrior ceremony? Why, you're crazy, Yamino-Kwiti! Our people have always had a warrior ceremony!"

"Yes, I know," said Yamino-Kwiti, "but nettles and ants are not enemies! And we don't let our enemies torture us if we can help it! So why should we let the ants?"

"Go away from me, Yamino-Kwiti," said Muka-Ayoin, whose state of mind could not follow the reasoning of the child. "Go away. You are crazy to think of changing the ways of our people! Are you afraid? Are you a coward that you speak so?"

"No!" answered Yamino-Kwiti. He rose to his feet. He no longer desired to comfort Muka-Ayoin. He was angry now.

No, he was not a coward. He would learn to scalp his enemies when the time came, but that did not mean he would ever like red ants. He could hear the men laughing and whooping and feasting. The older men were having a good time now that they had initiated more warriors into their group.

Yamino-Kwiti listened for a few moments, then went slowly to look at some of the old scalps hanging in Siba-vik's hut. He knew from the stories told about the fires at night that there were warlike enemies more cruel and merciless than his own people. He knew that some lived across the mountains far to the north, some in the desert to the

east beyond where the wind gods lived, and some
to the far south. Yet, in spite of this, he wanted
to see them, fight them, and conquer them and
their country. He put his hand up to his own hair
and felt his scalp. How would he feel without it?
Well, he'd be so great a warrior no Indian would
get his scalp! He squared his shoulders and left
the hut of Siba-vik, strutting like the cock quail,
only to come face to face with Pul Maat. Each time
he determined on an adventurous career, he came
against Pul Maat. That man was becoming the
very symbol of disappointment to him.

"Come with me, Yamino-Kwiti," he said. "Today you learn the rain song of our people."

"But I know the rain song," protested Yamino-
Kwiti. "It goes this way:

"Hid the season in the water for the sky was dry,
Came the wild geese from the water flying high,
Took with them drops of water on their wings——"

"That is not the rain song!" interrupted Pul
Maat. "Where did you learn that?"

"It is *my* rain song, Pul Maat," said Yamino-
Kwiti. "It sings itself in my head."

"*Nio mare!* What a child!" said Pul Maat.

"Look!" said Yamino-Kwiti pointing to the
southeast. "My rain song brings the rain! There
it comes!"

Pul Maat turned toward the southeast. A fresh
wind blew, and the smell of rain came to their
nostrils. Far off toward Wachbit the clouds had

come down to the earth, and the wind blew cool and damp.

"It looks like a storm!" said Pul Maat.

"I knew the rain would come," said Yamino-Kwiti, "because last night Moar, the moon, was taking a bath!"

Pul Maat grunted and wondered how it had happened that he, a *Pul*, had not seen the ring around the moon last night, the sign telling the Indians when Moar took a bath.

As they gazed a few drops fell on their upturned faces. All over the village came the cry: "Here comes the rain!" Pul Maat gave Yamino-Kwiti a puzzled look and then ran for shelter, since he had on a gorgeous feathered headdress. Most of the villagers did not mind the rain, for it felt good on their bare skins. The women wore no clothes other than grass skirts, while both men and women wore fur capes in the very cold weather. But when the cloudy darkness was suddenly split asunder by a flash of lightning, with an accompanying great roar from Tauwaro, the thunder, they fled like frightened children to their huts. They feared Taquich and Tauwaro[21] and hid themselves, huddling in a close circle about the fires in their wickiups.

The lightning and thunder soon ceased, but the wind blew, and the rain came down in a steady torrent. It was cozy and warm inside the huts, and thin plumes of smoke curled upward through

the holes in the top of each house, the insides of
which were black from the smoke which did not
escape.

The villagers soon began to make merry with
their favorite games and much loud laughter,
while the rain beat steadily against the grass sides
of the huts.

Pul Maat hung his headdress on a twig that had
not been trimmed from the willow poles forming
the framework of his house.  He sat on his heels
before the little fire in the center of the floor.  He
was troubled.  Had Yamino-Kwiti's rain song anything to do with this unusually heavy downpour?
Who and what was this child whom he had begun
to train and subdue?  His simple Indian mind could
not understand a child whose ambitions did not
include the sacred *Puplum!*

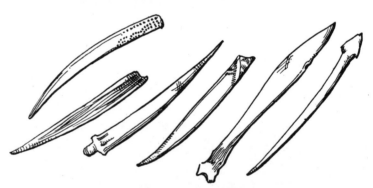

Men's hair ornaments or bone hairpins.

At the sound of a voice, Muka-Ayoin sat up suddenly.

Saor, Kwawar, and Tobet.

# 17

## Two Prayers to Kwawar

OR THREE DAYS Tamít, the sun, hid himself behind a thick, wet sky. The rain continued steadily. The river running past Siba flowed swift and full, leaving the riverbed and spreading over the wash. Little pools of water stood in all the hollows of the little village, and rivulets ran in unaccustomed places, even into some of the wickiups.

The Rain Makers among the *Puplum* were troubled. What part of their ceremonies had been overdone to produce this unexpected deluge? They gathered together in the shelter of Pul Maat's hut and talked it over, and Pul Maat reluctantly told them of the rain song of Yamino-Kwiti. Could it be possible that the child had magic powers? It had been a long time since the tribe had had a natural magician. Most of them had been taught by the *Puplum* and the medicine men and had acquired their art by diligent practice. Yamino-Kwiti must be held in bounds. Pul Maat was advised by Pul Eraxbu and the others to subdue him as quickly as possible, lest Siba be washed away.

Pul Maat left his fellow counselors and went into the pouring rain to find Yamino-Kwiti. He made the rounds of the village, peering into each hut as he passed it, into those of Mamish-Ahikañ, Koti-Cuit, and the one where little Kihut-Kiur lived, but Yamino-Kwiti was nowhere to be seen.

He saw other children going in and out, unmindful of the rain on their naked little bodies. They were splashing through the small pools, rolling in the soft mud, wading in the wash where the river eddies swirled along the banks, and then crawling into the huts to get dry and warm. The women kept the fires going inside and were busy about their tasks.

He could hear the men in the large hut which was used for councils and tribal gatherings in cold and wet weather. They were very noisy, and Pul Maat knew from the sounds of hilarity that the men were playing their favorite game of *Churchurki.*[40] Dignified and stern as he was, he could not resist the temptation of joining them. Besides, he said to himself, it was possible that Yamino-Kwiti might be where he had no business being—watching the grownups.

*Churchurki* was an exciting game, and the men of Siba played it with an intense enthusiasm. Pul Maat had no sooner wormed his way into the perspiring crowd around the players when he, too, caught the contagion of excitement and was soon betting as lively as the others. He forgot that he had started to find Yamino-Kwiti.

All through the game the paid singers sang to

the accompaniment of shrill whistles on bone pipes and flutes. Since they were paid for their services they did their best to earn their wages by making as much noise as possible.

Amid the tumult of the orchestra could be heard the voice of the umpire. He was paid to keep count, to prevent cheating, and to supply the firewood.

The players themselves, sitting on the ground in two rows of four facing each other, made no sound. They passed the little white *Churchurki* stick from one hand to another with practiced dexterity, and the onlookers grew frenzied in their betting as to who had it. Some so lost themselves in their excitement they wagered away their entire possessions. When this happened, some of them got rash enough to wager away the only thing they had left—their wives!

While all this hilarity was going on in the big hut, Muka-Ayoin and Yamino-Kwiti, who was unaware of the scare he had given the *Puplum*, had taken advantage of the rising water in the marshes and had constructed a snare among the water grasses to catch the waterfowl.

Each of them had a special purpose for gathering the beautiful feathers of the wild ducks. Muka-Ayoin had not forgotten the Indian girl, Kicha-Shungal. He needed feathers to make himself attractive so that he might gain favor in her eyes. Besides, had he not successfully gone through the warrior's ceremony? He would need a warrior's headgear and ceremonial skirt. Already he had acquired the necessary eagle feathers for the headdress.

Yamino-Kwiti wanted feathers for quite a different purpose. He had been forming a plan to evade Pul Maat and his insistent training without disobeying. He had decided to make a prayer offering to Kwawar. All the feathers of the condor which he had caught with Puku-Kakar had been used by the *Puplum*, but these duck feathers were his own.

With the ducks slung over their shoulders the boys returned home through the rain. Their hair was soaked with rainwater which ran down their backs in little rivulets, but they did not notice it. In fact, they liked the water on their skin, until the wind came up and it turned colder. Then they shivered and hurried to get to the village and the warm fires inside the huts.

As they reached the outskirts of the village they could hear the uproar of the *Churchurki* players, and Muka-Ayoin hurried to deposit his ducks in a safe place before joining the game. But Yamino-Kwiti knew that he would not be allowed inside the place, which was already overcrowded with noisy spectators and was as hot and stuffy as the sweathouse,[41] so he went to his hut.

No one was there, but the fire was smoldering in the firehole in the center of the floor. He put more wood on till it blazed a little and lighted the dark, smoky interior. Amid the distant shouts of the gamblers and the noise of the orchestra, he could hear the drip, drip, drip under the big oak outside the hut and the sough of the wind through wet branches. Occasionally a few raindrops came through the smoke hole in the top of the wickiup and hissed into the fire.

As he knelt beside the fire its light reflected on his serious young face. He stripped the feathers from the ducks and took the bodies outdoors to cover completely with mud. He put them into the hot ashes and covered them over in one corner of the firehole. They would be cooking while he made the prayer offerings.

Going to the tule mat on which he slept and turning one corner aside, he dug away the dirt until he uncovered several stones, little sparkling pieces of quartz that he had found along the river-bed one day and had carried home to treasure. He took three pieces of deerskin and put some of the stones in each one, tied them up with willow bast, and, drying the feathers until they were fluffy and bright, tucked them in between the strands until each object looked like a feathered ball. He smiled as he worked, for he was contented with his handicraft and was sure that the Great Spirit would be also.

It was only recently that Pul Maat had instructed him regarding the three forms of Kwawar.[11] Yamino-Kwiti decided that if there were three of Him then there must be three offerings.

Gathering his gifts in his arms, he crept out of the wickiup and found that the rain had ceased. The stars were twinkling brightly through the rifts in the clouds as they passed over the face of the moon. He could hear the gamblers still at their game, and from other huts came the crooning of lullabies as the grandmothers soothed the babies.

He ran silently and quickly through the mud to the dripping, wet *Yoba*, and in the cold starlight knelt before the wooden image of Kwawar. He placed his offerings on the ground before the idol and breathed softly, almost inaudibly: "Oh, Kwawar, see what I have brought for You! Are they not *cabatcho?*" He blew on the objects to make the feathers flutter, that they might attract the attention of Kwawar. In the strange language which only the *Puplum* used he whispered softly the incantation he had learned: *"Nom im manoc, im manoc; nom im manoc, im manoc, Yobarse!"*

Stretching out flat in the mud he touched the first ball with his fingers lightly. "Oh, Saor, this is for You—You who cannot dance, yet who lives within all things." He picked up the second ball in his hands and, getting to his feet, performed a part of the ceremonial dance of Tobet. "This one, Tobet," he said, "is for You. Is it not *cabatcho?*" The third and largest ball he took in his hands and lifted it toward the skies, whispering, "Oh,

Kwawar, see my gift! Oh, Great Giver of Life, make me a courier that I may go to strange places —Oh, make me a courier!" Letting his voice sink to a mere breath of a whisper, he said, "Kwawar! Kwawar! Make me a courier!"

Squatting on his heels, he looked up at the cloudy heavens above him . Why could he never see Kwawar who lived with the stars? He peered intently into the black depths of the sky between the drifting clouds and wondered. He heard feet splashing through the puddles not far away and silently hid himself behind the *Yoba* fence in the shadow. It was Pul Maat, muttering to himself in an angry undertone as he passed the *Yoba* on his way to his own hut.

Yamino-Kwiti began to feel very, very guilty. He had gone over the head of Pul Maat, as it were, to obtain the help of the Giver of Life. This was a function of the *Puplum*, the mediators between the Great Spirit and the people. Yamino-Kwiti was not yet a *Pul;* he was not even a *Púmal,* yet he had gone to the *Yoba* and petitioned Kwawar on his own account. Well, it was done now, and he would wait and see what the effect would be.

Pul Maat had passed on. Yamino-Kwiti had heard his angry mutterings and was filled with dread of him. Silently he crept out of the *Yoba* and slipped like a fleeting shadow across the wet earth and through the puddles to his own hut. He stood still a moment, listening to the laughter, shouts, and noise of the orchestra and the *Churchurki* players in the big hut in the center of the little village. He knew he would not be permitted to watch and that the game probably would be kept up all night, so he crawled into his own wickiup.

He uncovered the ducks from the hot ashes and found the mud case thoroughly dry and beginning to crack in some places. The ducks were done. Opening up the mud case, he laid them out to cool —for no Indian likes to eat hot food—and the fragrance of roasted duck filled the hut.

When he had finished his meal he added fuel to the low-burning fire and lay down for the night. Outside, the trees were still dripping—drip, drip, drip. Off in the distance he could hear Itaru crying to the night. "Perhaps," he said to himself, "Itaru is asking something of Y-yo-ha-rivg-nain, too."

Thinking of the beauty of his prayer offerings as they fluttered in the *Yoba* before the image of Kwawar and confident that somehow he would be relieved from having to be a *Pul*, he fell asleep.

In the meantime Pul Maat was fuming in his hut. He had forgotten that the rest of the *Puplum* had sent him to subdue his pupil, Yamino-Kwiti, and had fallen to the temptation of the game of *Churchurki*. He had bet as rashly as any of them and at first had amassed considerable of his companions' possessions. But his luck had suddenly changed, and, before he could realize his misfortune, he had wagered away everything he possessed. The very last thing had been his gorgeous headgear, and when he saw the delighted smile of old Wikuam who won it, he felt the humiliating defeat of all gamblers who lose. He could no longer stay and enjoy the game. Working his way through the crowd, he got into the open air and discovered that it was starlight and the rain was over! Muttering to himself, he went fuming to his own hut.

When he met Yamino-Kwiti the next morning the hour was late. He had rested badly, and, seeing the boy full of youthful spirits and playing joyously with his playmates at the game of lance and ring, or *hararicuar*,* he let his mood get the better of him and called the boy to him in a harsh voice.

Yamino-Kwiti handed his lance to Puku-Kakar and followed the old man to his hut, his heart beating guiltily. For several hours Pul Maat drilled the boy in puzzling and difficult memory tests. So gruff and surly was he that Yamino-Kwiti's brave and merry spirit was more subdued than it ever had been before.

Pul Maat had not been unaware of Yamino-Kwiti's ambition and strong desire to see the world as a courier. Mamish-Ahikañ and Siba-vik both had spoken of it. Naturally, Pul Maat was not in favor of it. Yamino-Kwiti was one of the quickest and brightest of the children of the tribe. Pul Maat had set his heart stubbornly on keeping the boy for his own chosen profession. In his present

---

* Ha-ra-ree'-koo-ar.

state of peevishness he deliberately undertook to thwart Yamino-Kwiti by telling him some long, drawn-out tales of horrors about travelers and had him repeat them word for word.

He told of the notorious Indian who, like Yamino-Kwiti, had wanted to see the world and had gone north only to encounter a race of people who used magic in a really alarming manner to subdue their enemies. This traveler had gone so far north that he had found the place where the gray geese breed. The people had ears that reached their hips. Yamino-Kwiti perked up his own ears at this bit of information. The old man allowed his imagination to get the better of him at this passage in the legend, for he told the child how the ears could stand out straight and hear *everything!* No one could approach, even silently, into their country, he said, but those huge, out-standing ears would hear him.

He told of the very perfect people who could, by just drawing in their breath, inhale the essence of food without bothering to prepare, chew, or eat it. Thus they were able to smell a rabbit or other animal and absorb it, throwing away with a disdainful gesture of the hand the part that was uneatable!

In his eagerness to tell the child all he knew of foreign lands, he made a mistake. He tried to intimidate the boy and thus keep him home. Instead, his efforts only served to make the child

more curious and desire more than ever to see
these strange people and their strange ways. He
was not afraid of their magic!

Pul Maat noticed that the boy's subdued and
obedient attitude when the lesson first began had
changed. When Yamino-Kwiti repeated the long
tale of the traveler his young voice was vibrant
with excitement. There was no fear in him!

Yamino-Kwiti had forgotten that he had run
from Hunar the first time he encountered her face
to face and that he had followed the river down
to the village because he was afraid of Itaru. He
remembered only when he had been brave. He
had faced Hunar on the trail and protected Kihut-
Kiur, he had caught a condor which was a man's
task, and he had helped to capture enemies twice
in one summer. He remembered only his brave
defiance of danger as an Indian boy should, so why
would he fear a race of people in the far north?

Pul Maat, however, had no intention of allowing an adventurous spirit to thrive under his
teaching. He would find some way to frustrate it,
he said to himself. When the lesson was over,
therefore, he went to his own wickiup. Sitting
cross-legged before his fire, he pondered deeply on
the subject for the rest of the day. He filled his
pipe with wild tobacco. As its smoke mingled with
the smoke of the fire he muttered in the sacred
language incantations to conjure up spirits of
long-dead wizards and others of the *Puplum* to

confer with them. If he were powerless to conquer
the ambitious nature of Yamino-Kwiti, he would
call on the invisible powers and gods to help him!
He would use his magic to some purpose!

When he finally emerged from his wickiup, it
was dark. All the rest of the villagers were asleep,
for the game of *Churchurki* had at last come to
an end. He stood with his arms folded and gazed
at the stars shining above him in the cold, dark sky.
Turning to the north star, he said, "Ah, Rómi, you
who never move, watch me! I shall subdue Yamino-
Kwiti with the Toloache\* ceremony! He shall be
ours!"

Lifting his arms high above his head, he gave
a stamp and a jump in the direction of Fúmi, the
north; then a stamp and a jump toward Crúmi, the
east; another toward Kitúmi, the south; and lastly
toward Páymi, the west, chanting in a singsong
voice his prayer to the invisible powers of Nature
—the world in which he lived.

> Do You see me, Kwawar?
> Do You see me, Saor?
> Do You see me, Tobet?
> Do You all help me!
> *O-a nahucua*, Fúmi!
> *O-a nahacua*, Crúmi!
> *O-a nahacua*, Kitúmi!
> *O-a nahacua*, Páymi!
> Do You all help me!
> And You, Tamít,

---

\* Tō-lō-à'-che.

And You, Moar!
*O-a nahacua*, all of You!
Enter Thou in the heart of Yamino-Kwiti!
All of You, *O-a nahacua!*
Make him a priest to his people!
All of You, *O-a nahacua!*

With face lifted to the stars and arms upraised he stood for many moments, and then silently, slowly, he turned and entered his hut, certain that all the powers of the invisible were in accord with him and against Yamino-Kwiti's cherished ambition.

But the gods had other plans for the gay and adventurous spirit of Yamino-Kwiti.

A feather headdress.

# 18

# The Wedding of Muka-Ayoin

PUL MAAT was disappointed about the Toloache ceremony. When Tamít, the sun, began his slow journey to his house in the south and the days grew shorter and shorter, the wind and the rain combined with the cold to make a long, wet winter. So the Toloache ceremony was postponed.

When spring came all the world was carpeted with flowers, and bees gathered honey in the chaparral, birds sang among the new green leaves of the trees, and other and gayer activities than Toloache ceremonies absorbed the people of Siba.

Yamino-Kwiti was awakened early one morning by laughter and commotion in the village. People were calling to one another, and the young men and women were laughing and shouting. Yamino-Kwiti threw aside his rabbitskin blanket and crawled out of the door of the hut. It was not yet light, in that translucent grey of early dawn, and the air was cool. It was the time of year when the trees were sprouting forth bright new leaves. There was a blithe and merry feeling everywhere.

"What is it?" Yamino-Kwiti asked his mother, who was busy at the outdoor fire. "Why are they laughing?" He hugged himself to keep from

Pul Maat conjures up spirits of long-dead wizards.

With mincing, dancing steps the party approached.

shivering, for the early mornings were still cool.

"Have you forgotten, Little Runner?" she asked him. "Today the youngest of your father's brothers, Muka-Ayoin, takes a wife. There will be a feast and much dancing. Have you forgotten all the gifts that you and your father with Koti-Cuit and all the kinfolk took to your uncle's house at the new of the moon? Don't you remember the long strings of money beads and the skins of foxes, rabbits, and deer that we gave to the family of the bride?"

"I remember," said Yamino-Kwiti. "And they gave us seeds and chia meal. Is it the little thin one from Yangna, or the fat one that he marries?"

A woman's grass skirt worn in front. Knobs of asphalt hang at the ends to keep the strands from flying in the wind.

"*Alala!* Not the fat one, nor the thin one from Yangna," laughed his mother. "It is the slim *cabatcho* from Asuksa!" Shaking her head at him, she added, "What is the matter with your memory, Yamino-Kwiti, that you forget?"

Yamino-Kwiti laughed. "I have not forgotten the *cabatcho* from Asuksa," he said. "That is Kitcha-Shungal." And he told his mother again how Muka-Ayoin had killed the panther when it was about to leap upon the Indian girl.

"What a good thing it is not the fat one from Yangna," laughed his mother. "Your father would not enjoy the thought of carrying the fat one even for Muka-Ayoin. It is enough to carry the thin one from halfway to your uncle's house."

"Why must he carry her?" asked Yamino-Kwiti, whose curiosity never seemed satisfied.

"Ah, silly one, why indeed," sniffed his mother. "Is it not because he is the strongest of all his kinfolk, and the strongest man carries the bride?"

A boyish voice from down by the river called out, "Yamino-Kwiti, Yamino-Kwiti! Come on!"

"There go Tomear and Puku-Kakar," he said. "Coming!" he shouted, and he ran to join the other boys in the water. In they all plunged, puffing and blowing and splashing as small boys do when they get into cold water.

The Indian boys did not go into the water to get clean, for they had no thought about being dirty, since they lived so close to the good earth. But each night the funny little *Mututci*,⁴³ or hopping fleas, would seek shelter in the warm huts and would gather in great numbers to bite and pester the sleepers until they were glad to run to the river in the morning to wash them off.

"We have to fill our baskets with seeds and berries for the wedding," said Puku-Kakar, with only his head showing out of the water. "My mother has that many baskets to fill," and he held up his two hands with all ten wet fingers spread wide.

"I know how many that is," said Tomear; "that is *wehés mahar*,⁴⁴ because this one is *mahar*," and Tomear spread the fingers on one hand, "and this is *wehés mahar*." He held up both hands.

"Let's hurry," said Puku-Kakar. "Here comes Puy-Puy. When we all scramble for the seeds at the wedding today, you watch him."

Amid the sounds of revelry someone was calling from the village: "Children! Come!"

"Listen, they are calling us!" said Tomear. "Come on!"

"Wait for me!" cried Puy-Puy, as the other boys ran out of the water, slapping themselves as they ran, to get dry.

"Coming, coming!" they shouted. Puy-Puy was forced either to stay behind or go without his bath, and, being a rather lazy little boy, he did the latter.

When Yamino-Kwiti reached his father's hut he found that his mother had hung garlands of flowers about her neck, and had all their baskets filled with seeds, dried berries, wild cherries, piñon nuts, and acorns. This was not the season for seeds and berries, and so they must take them from the huge storage baskets, or *chamucas*, which stood higher than Yamino-Kwiti's head.

"How fast you work, Mother," said Yamino-Kwiti.

"Oh, no," answered his mother, "I did not do it all. I had help. See, there is my helper," and she pointed to the end of the willow-pole fence which extended as a windbreak part way around their hut.

Yamino-Kwiti heard a merry laugh behind him, and, whirling on his feet, he saw a laughing, dimpled, little brown face peering at him from around the end of the fence.

"Kihut-Kiur!" cried Yamino-Kwiti. "Come out here!"

Kihut-Kiur came laughing and dancing into the enclosure. Like all the other children, on this festive day, she was covered from head to foot with flowers. Long strings of blue brodiaea hung about her little brown neck with garlands of baby-blue eyes and creamcups. A skirt of blue and purple lupines was fastened around her waist, while on her head was a crown of golden poppies.

"Oh!" said Yamino-Kwiti, with a smile of pleasure. "It is Kihut-Kiur who is *cabatcho* now, Mother."

"Yes," said his mother, smiling at the two children. "Watch well, you two, at the wedding today of Muka-Ayoin and the *cabatcho* from Asuksa. Someday when you two are old enough it will be the same with you that it is with them. So it was promised by the father of Kihut-Kiur to your father, Yamino-Kwiti."

"Will you wear flowers and a crown just like that, Kihut-Kiur?" asked Yamino-Kwiti.

"Oh, yes," answered the little girl, "but many, many more! And there will be many money beads about my neck. My father and mother have said that I am worth many *sayako* now, and by the time I am old enough there will have to be a great big pile!"

Kihut-Kiur raised herself up on her tiptoes and, stretching her hands as high as they could go, showed Yamino-Kwiti the height of the pile of money beads that might be a part of the gifts given in exchange when she should be old enough to marry.

Yamino-Kwiti shouted, "You couldn't wear *that* many about your neck, Kihut-Kiur, or they would crush you like this!" and Yamino-Kwiti fell flat on the earth with an Indian grunt. Kihut-Kiur giggled.

Before he could get up his father appeared. "Come, all of you. We are ready to start." Yamino-Kwiti scrambled to his feet.

His mother lifted the baskets to the shoulders of the little girl and herself, crushing some of the flowers in their garlands as she did so, and off they went to meet with the rest of the relatives of the groom.

Muka-Ayoin stood tall and proud, with strings of shell beads about his neck, shell rings from his ears, a feathered headdress upon his head, and his face and body painted gaily with white and blue horizontal stripes. He stood laughing among his relatives. All was ready, and the party formed in line, Mamish-Ahikañ advancing before the other relatives, while the groom retired into his own wickiup to await the return of the party with the bride.

It was a long line of relatives which followed the tall, strong figure of the chief's courier. He took the trail toward Asuksa with a mincing, dancing step, which all the others copied. Men relatives went first, then the women, and after them the children, covered with garlands of flowers. A great crowd of villagers trailed along in the rear with much banter and laughter.

The whole light-stepping, slowly advancing procession sang and chanted as they went forward until the bride's party came into sight on the trail, when a great shout went up. Both parties danced forward until the courier was opposite the man who carried the bride high on his shoulder. The two tall men exchanged the burden amid a shower of blossoms, and now it was Mamish-Ahikañ who carried her perched on his shoulder, her slender bare feet hanging down to be grasped by the strong hands of the courier.

She was decked in finery; strings of beads— blue, black, and white—hung about her neck. Her dress, instead of the usual grass skirt, was one of deerskin heavily ornamented with birds' feathers and tiny glistening shells, while her cheeks were painted a bright red. Oh, she was gay and beautiful—*cabatcho*, as Yamino-Kwiti said.

With the same mincing, dancing steps the party now approached the hut where the groom waited for his bride. The company following broke ranks and with lavish hands threw a shower of seeds from the baskets over the bride as she was placed beside her husband in the newly constructed hut. The scramble now began for the villagers, and such a noise and confusion ensued that the children were often rolled over and over as the stronger ones grabbed and gathered the seeds and nuts, laughing and shouting.

All the pretty flowers with which the little girls and the women had decked themselves were crushed and broken, but what did it matter? The seeds which had been thrown over the couple by the relatives for good fortune and good health were scattered on the ground and must be picked up— to the last seed—for they were very precious.

Yamino-Kwiti and Puku-Kakar bumped heads in the scramble. The two boys laughed and rubbed the bumped places. "Watch Puy-Puy," whispered

Puku-Kakar. Puy-Puy was on his knees with his
basket held tightly in his teeth so that he might
reach with both hands at once for the seeds and
nuts on the ground.

"Now watch me," said Puku-Kakar. He picked
up a large stone, and, going stealthily behind Puy-
Puy, he reached over his head and dropped the
stone into Puy-Puy's basket. The sudden weight
tore it out of his teeth, and the seeds spilled all
over the ground again. Greedy little Puy-Puy
wasted no time in crying about his loss; he picked
up his basket and went to work again, faster than
ever, while the other children laughed and teased.

By the time the seeds had all been regathered,
the party was hungry and it was time for the feast.
Again the women were busy, while the men made

Burden-bearer.

merry. They had done their part the day before when there had been a great hunt. They had stalked the deer and the antelope, bringing their game home with much rejoicing and shouting. It was the women's work to cook the meat and keep the fires going.

The feast lasted far into the night, with games and dancing, until the children were weary. Ya-mino-Kwiti and Kihut-Kiur fell asleep, their stomachs nearly bursting, but the men and women seemed never to stop. When Yamino-Kwiti was roused much later by his mother he could hear them still chanting, singing, and dancing. He saw the long, grotesque, bobbing shadows thrown by the fire along the ground until they merged into the outer darkness that surrounded the little village of Siba.

# 19

# The Mysterious Toloache

AMINO-KWITI and Tomear were watching with considerable anxiety the construction of a brush enclosure. It was late, and the sun had set in a blaze of color. Indifferent to the glory of the still glowing sky, they sat on the green grass and watched the men complete the brush fence. They were forming a temporary *Yoba*, which was the smaller of two. The larger *Yoba* had been finished first, and the spectators were already gathering there to sit cross-legged about the fire, awaiting events. Pul Maat had at last had his way, and not only Yamino-Kwiti, but all the comrades near his age were to undergo the *Toloache* ceremony as soon as the stars began to shine.

"I'm terribly hungry; aren't you, Tomear?" said Yamino-Kwiti, putting both hands on his stomach, which was uncomfortably flat.

"Yes, I am," agreed Tomear, "and so are the other boys; but we can't eat until this is ended." The other boys were enduring a self-imposed torture by hovering about the cooking fires, where food gave forth a tantalizing aroma—tantalizing because the boys could have none of it.

"I'll be glad when it is over," continued Yamino-Kwiti. "But just the same, I don't like being a *Púmal.*"

"But," argued Tomear, "you must have a protector! If you don't, all kinds of things could happen to you when you hunt!"

"Yes, I know," said Yamino-Kwiti, listlessly lying back on the grass. "Y-yo-ha-rivg-nain cannot be seen as a protector except when he shows himself as an animal in a vision—but, Tomear!" Yamino-Kwiti sat up suddenly. "Is he *all* the animals? Or just the ones we see when we drink the *Toloache?*"

Tomear looked solemn and scratched his head. He could not answer Yamino-Kwiti. "I don't know," he finally admitted. "Let us ask my father. Here he comes now with the other boys."

Siba-vik was accompanied by Akura-vik, who was to be the officiating chief in the ceremony. It was the custom to call in a chief of another village on such occasions. Akura-vik walked with an important swagger, his necklaces swinging with his stride and making little clicking noises.

The other boys were following behind. They were a hungry-looking group of boys, as lacking in animation and as flat of stomach as Yamino-Kwiti and Tomear. They all knew they would be a good deal hungrier before the affair was completed, and were striving desperately to be stoical about it.

Tomear did not have an opportunity to ask Siba-vik about the all-pervading presence in animals of Y-yo-ha-rivg-nain, for directly behind the boys came the sponsors—old men, among whom were Pul Maat, Pul Eraxbu, Wikuam, Sacasca-Tatma, and Grandfather. Behind the old men came the old women, who would also act as attendants.

There was a ceremonious air of mystery about the older people that filled the boys with a nervous uneasiness which they tried to hide, but without much success.

The brush *Yoba* was completed, and, as the stars were one by one peeping out of the darkening heavens, torches were lighted. The drinking of *Toloache* was about to begin.

The strange liquid had already been prepared by the medicine men with muttered, magical words. They made it from the powdered dry leaves of the *pibat*, or datura plant. But only these dealers in magic knew with what other ingredients it was mixed to make it so potent that the drinker would have a vision of an otherwise invisible power. Kwawar would come, as a protector, they were told, in various forms of animals, and each candidate must be careful to observe the actions and the probable advice of the vision.

A feeling of depression and helplessness came over Yamino-Kwiti when he found that Pul Maat was to be his sponsor, but he went with the old man into the enclosure with a dutiful meekness.

He allowed that determined individual to hold the small mortar containing the *Toloache* with one hand and his forehead with the other while he drank the mysterious concoction.

He wanted chokingly to spit it all out, but he did not dare, with the small black eyes of Pul Maat shining at him in the light of the torches, and the flickering shadows all about him like so many eerie representatives from the invisible world.

As soon as each boy had drunk his share of the *Toloache*, he was led to the other and larger enclosure, where the people were already beginning the dancing and singing. The fire threw a wavering light on the high cheekbones and painted bodies of the dancers. The boys began to feel strangely; the dancers took on grotesque shapes; and the songs sounded now near, now far away. The words made no sense at all except the ones which kept repeating: "The *Toloache* bowl walks twisting, twisting! The people dance writhing, writhing!"

Sometimes Yamino-Kwiti thought the earth was going to drop from under his feet. Sometimes it seemed to come up and hit him, and all through the strange dancing in the weird firelight and shifting shadows he could feel Pul Maat holding him so he would not fall. The old man constantly warned, in his bearlike voice: "Keep awake! Keep awake! If you go to sleep you'll not see your protector! Keep awake!"

Some of the boys could not withstand the over-powering drowsiness and slumped, unconscious, into the arms of their sponsors. When this happened, the sponsor picked up the boy and, with his relaxed body in his arms, or thrown across his shoulder, continued the dancing and chanting around the fire. Others were carried out to the smaller *Yoba* and left in the charge of old men or women, who did their best to waken and to keep awake the candidate, who otherwise would be denied his vision.

The people continued their dancing through the night. It was a time of magic, of mysterious influences, and the people danced with frenzy. They stopped only to watch the medicine men perform their magic feats. A-nub-su-voi-rot swallowed his wooden sword and retrieved it without any particular difficulty. Several of the medicine men allowed themselves to be shot with arrows, recovering from their severe wounds so quickly and completely that all who saw were convinced of their supernatural qualities and their divine knowledge.

For several days the mad mysteries were prolonged. The boys were not allowed to eat or sleep, but sleepiness and hunger were not all they had to endure, for their fortitude and endurance were put to the test in many ways.

One by one they saw their longed-for vision. Yamino-Kwiti was swaying on his tired legs, and Pul Maat stood in front of him exhorting him to keep awake. So bearlike was his voice that suddenly Yamino-Kwiti saw, between firelight and shadows, his sponsor's figure change form. He was unexpectedly Hunar standing on hind legs and wagging a huge head over Yamino-Kwiti. Pul Maat's voice became Hunar's roar, and Yamino-Kwiti, unable to get away on his unstable legs, cried out, "Hunar, Hunar!" and fell unconscious at Pul Maat's feet.

But the ceremony was not over, even after the boys had seen their visions. There was more to be done. A sand painting[45] of colored sands had been made in the center of the large *Yoba*. It represented the universe as the Indians knew it—porpoises swimming around the edge; seven giants holding the world on their shoulders; the sun, the moon, and the stars; those things which were a part of their daily life; dangerous animals, and those that spelled death to the Indians—tarantula, rattlesnake, bear, and mountain lion. This was the picture which Akura-vik used to illustrate the long speech he gave to all the boys. He told of the rules and laws of their tribe and the kind of punishment befalling those who broke them. He pointed with a dramatic finger to the animals who would avenge wrongdoing. It seemed to the tired brain of Yamino-Kwiti that he pointed to Hunar and dwelt with greater emphasis upon what Hunar would do than upon any of the other deadly or poisonous creatures.

After that came the chewing of sage meal mixed with salt. Each boy must chew and chew until the stuff was rolled into a sort of pellet. Leaning on both hands at the edge of the painting, with practiced aim they ejected the ill-tasting wad toward the hole in the middle of the sand painting. Akuravik observed with peering eyes the condition of each pellet. Should it be too moist, or not in the hole in the center, he declared that the spitter was heedless and unconcerned with the precepts and laws of the tribe, whereupon the spectators entered into the ceremony with vim, vigorously hooting their disapproval of the careless one.

The hungry boys were requested to perform one last detail of the ceremony. Three flat stones were laid in a row some distance apart. Between the second and the last one was a round hole. Each initiate was expected to step cautiously with the ball of his foot on the first stone, to hop onto the second, and leap over the hole to the third. Each boy in turn accomplished this feat excepting Puy-Puy, who, weak from hunger and sleepiness, slipped on the second stone and tumbled headfirst into the hole. A loud sound of horror and dismay came from the lips of the spectators, for such a catastrophe was regarded as an omen of a short life.

And now the boys could be fed. Shaking on their legs, they were led to the feast amid the barking of dogs, happy shouting of the smaller children,

He was unexpectedly Hunar standing on hind legs and wagging
a huge head over Yamino-Kwiti.

"He was bigger than this!"

and the crackling of fires from which the fragrance of wood smoke and cooking meat came to their sensitive nostrils. But the meat was not for the boys as yet.

The temporary *Yobas*, large and small, were destroyed, since their purpose had been served. The brush fences were heaped into a huge pile and burned.

The *Toloache* ceremony was over. Yamino-Kwiti was now a *Púmal*, with Hunar as a protector. But he began to wonder if Y-yo-ha-rivg-nain did not like his carefully made prayer offerings, for it seemed as though Pul Maat had had his way.

The toloache bowl and Datura plant.

# 20

# The Crows Make a Prediction

THE FOLLOWING afternoon the boys were lying on the soft green grass of the riverbank. They could head the activities of the village behind them, mothers crooning their lullabies to their babies, grandmothers scolding the small children for getting in the way. They could hear the laughter of the men at their storytelling and games. The boys were eating little dried cakes of acorn meal. They would not be allowed to eat meat for some time. But so hungry had they been all through the ceremony that they felt they would never again be full enough.

"Now we can be hunters like the men," said Puku-Kakar. "Only I never shall kill Tonar, the antelope buck, for he is my protector."

"Itaru is mine," said Tomear. "He will give me counsel as he does the *Puplum*, and I shall be a wise chief when I am a man!"

Yamino-Kwiti looked at Puy-Puy, waiting for him to speak, but Puy-Puy was silently digging little holes in the earth with his fingers.

"What did you see, Puy-Puy?" asked Yamino-Kwiti, "when the vision came?"

Puy-Puy scowled and sat up straight. The other boys were silent, waiting for him to tell the name of his protector.

"Did anyone ever see—Cuwot?"[46] he finally asked.

The other boys sat up too. "Cuwot?" they asked breathlessly. "Did you see Cuwot?"

"I don't know," Puy-Puy admitted miserably. "It must have been Cuwot, because he said 'Cu, cu' and flapped wings that were so big and black it couldn't have been anything else."

"But *no one* ever saw Cuwot! He is invisible!" exclaimed Tomear.

"What did he look like?" asked Wupu-Yatcho, doubt written on his face.

This intense interest of the other boys was very pleasant to Puy-Puy, who was usually laughed at because of his strange ways.

"He was as big—as big—as—bigger than this!" and Puy-Puy stretched his arms wide, "and taller than this!" He stood up, reaching his hands above his head. "His neck and head were red, and his body was black!"

"That sounds like Ashawut, the eagle," said Tomear.

"Or Panes, the condor," added Yamino-Kwiti.

"Does Ashawut say 'Cu, cu?'" asked Puy-Puy, contemptuously, thrusting his chin forward. "Or Panes, either?"

"No," and all the others shook their heads.

"But," argued Tomear again, "no one ever has seen Cuwot. They have only heard him in the night, and no one knows what he is." Tomear scowled at Puy-Puy. "If he is invisible how could *you* see him, Puy-Puy?"

"But, Tomear," said Yamino-Kwiti, "Y-yo-ha-rivg-nain is also invisible but can be seen in a vision. A vision is something only *one* can see."

"Did you tell the Elders it was Cuwot?" asked Puku-Kakar.

"No," answered Puy-Puy. "I thought it was Ashawut, the eagle, at first—and Siba-vik was glad for me—but, I don't think it was Ashawut, because Ashawut doesn't say 'Cu, cu' and isn't so big! The vision I saw was awful—and bigger and blacker than the night when the moon and the stars are gone!"

The boys were still for a moment, thinking. Then Puku-Kakar said in a frightened whisper, "Maybe it was Zizu,[47] the demon!"

They were all startled, and Puy-Puy cried out: "No, no! It wasn't Zizu! Zizu isn't an animal or a bird; he doesn't protect hunters!"

"Zizu," said Wupu-Yatcho, "is a demon from the desert. He can follow anyone by his scent, as a dog does."

Puy-Puy was almost ready to cry. By having seen so unusual a vision he had enjoyed a distinction among his playmates which he seldom had. Now his usual fate of unimportance was thrust upon him again by the suggestion that it was Zizu and not the mysterious bird Cuwot who had come to him in his vision and was to be his protector. He was plainly disheartened.

Yamino-Kwiti saw the distress of Puy-Puy and tactfully changed the subject. "My protector is Hunar!" he announced, solemnly. He did not know whether to be glad or sorry, for he had never quite forgotten the fright Hunar gave him when he almost rubbed noses with the bear at the honey tree. However, it was good to know that he would have the protection of Hunar. He would try now to think of Hunar with the reverence due a protector.

"It will be good for me, I think," said Puku-Kakar, "to stay close to you when we hunt." And all the boys laughed, except Puy-Puy.

A shadow flitted across the sunlit grass, and a black feather fell among the boys.

"Caw, caw!" said a raucous voice above them. In the sycamore branches was Akukuch, the crow. He seemed intensely interested in the group below him. He turned his head on one side and said again, "Caw, caw!" as though to give warning. Then suddenly flapping his wings he descended among the boys on the grass so unexpectedly that he managed to snatch the mealy morsel from the fingers of Tomear and fly away with it.

"*Nio mare!*" said Tomear. "That means a stranger comes among us!"

"Look!" cried Wupu-Yatcho, pointing to the south. "There are a whole flock of them!"

Suddenly the boys were surrounded by so many of the little black rascals that they hid their food behind their backs and, lying on the ground, kicked their feet and waved their legs and shouted at the dusky thieves. The whole flock flew, cawing, to scatter themselves over a near-by patch of wild grapevines. They seemed to be indignant at such treatment. The women did not defend themselves in such a fashion from the crows, but sat silent and still when they came like little black robbers to grab the food from their very hands. But the boys were hungry and had no intention of giving up that which they had waited so long to get.

The courier.

"If one crow means a stranger coming," said Yamino-Kwiti, "what does a whole flock of them mean?"

"It must mean a whole lot of strangers," said Puku-Kakar. The boys looked at each other, suddenly solemn.

"I wonder," said Tomear, "if they are friends or enemies."

"They would not be strangers if they were friends," said Yamino-Kwiti. "Come, I'm going to tell my father."

# 21

## Yamino-Kwiti Meets the Strangers

THREE LITTLE girls, Manisar, Ki-hut-Kiur, and Chukít, the little sister of Puku-Kakar, were picking flowers in the fields. Their arms were full of the bright-colored blossoms that bloom so profusely during the Green Grass Moon, the month of sunshine and showers. They had woven soft, dainty garlands of the little gold and brown violets that covered the shady slopes with a woody fragrance, fashioned fancy skirts of the long blossoms of the sky-blue lupine, and woven crowns of suncups and lilac lilies. They sat now in the green grass and chattered like magpies, their little brown fingers busy with the flowers.

It was here that the boys found them. Nothing would do but that Kihut-Kiur should drape her garlands about the neck of Yamino-Kwiti, who laughed and pranced with delight. Manisar put her gay, floral crown on the black head of her brother Tomear, who said it was a queer kind of a war bonnet for a chief. It was sunny and warm in the field, and the children were happy, laughing and chattering as only children can, when Yamino-Kwiti suddenly realized it was getting dark.

"Look!" he cried. "The sky animal is swallowing Tamít!"

Dropping the lovely flowers, the children, both boys and girls, ran with all their might to the village, scattering blossoms as they ran. There they found the village folk just as frightened as they were. Some of the people were shouting at the top of their lungs. They were trying to frighten the dragon who lived in the sky and who endeavored to swallow the sun or the moon every now and then. They held their deerhides aloft and beat them with sticks, making a resounding slap, slap, slap! They swung a noisy *mom-lah-pish,* or bull-roarer; they clattered their split-board rattle and threw sand and pebbles at the sky and kept up a continual din and tumult until finally the darkness gradually left them, and the sun little by little resumed its brightness.

Then the other Indians who had been too frightened to shout, and who had crawled into their huts or down among the willows, came out of hiding and tried to keep from trembling, but the old men of the *Puplum* strutted about in lordly fashion. Had they not forced the dragon to disgorge his prey? Look! There was Tamít as good as ever, and the dragon had disappeared. They were mighty men, these wizards, and the people praised them.

A few days after this event a runner came into the village seeking Siba-vik. He was a stranger from the country to the south.

"See!" said Tomear to Yamino-Kwiti. "The crows told us! Here is the stranger!"

"Yes, but where is the flock of strangers that the crows told about?" Yamino-Kwiti asked, and Tomear shrugged his shoulders.

The chief was not in his hut, and Yamino-Kwiti was sent to find him. The runner, in the meantime, managed to get his breath so that when Siba-vik arrived, with Yamino-Kwiti at his heels, he was able to tell his message without panting.

There were strange white men, he said, in the Indian country far to the south in Nipawai.[8] They had come from out of the sea in a great winged house when the dragon swallowed the sun! They had camped on the shore, and many of them were sick.

"That must be the flock of strangers," said Tomear.

"Then they must be coming here," said Yamino-Kwiti. The two boys looked at each other with expectation and curiosity in their faces.

"Did you see them?" asked Siba-vik of the courier.

"No," answered the stranger, "I did not see them. A runner like myself came from Nipawai telling the news to each hamlet on the way. He was so spent when he arrived that another runner from Wiawio[8] carried the message to my village, Ahachmai,[8] from where I have just come, sent by my chief."

The stranger was rested and fed before he returned to Ahachmai, while Mamish-Ahikañ was sent by Siba-vik to tell the news to Asuksa, Kukomo, Wachbit, and other hamlets to the east.

In all his ten years, Yamino-Kwiti had not known such excitement as now prevailed in Siba. All the narratives of other white men coming out of the sea in "winged whales," in days of long ago, were told and retold. With each telling these strange beings gained characteristics that were weird and supernatural. They were like remote gods come from the sea, and nothing real was known about them. It was rumored, however, among the people of Siba and other Indian villages, that there were some of these strange beings far beyond the mountains to the east where lived the demon, Taquich, in his canyon, and the mystery of those faraway people added to the mystery of these strangers. Did they not live beyond the home of the wind gods and Tauwaro, the thunder? Were they, then, gods, too, come in person?

All through the summer moons of Tocoboaich and Sintecar,[12] there were reports of the white men in the southern bay of Nipawai. Another "winged whale" had brought more white men, and others had come to join them at Nipawai from the country farther south where lived enemies of their tribe. Much of the enmity, however, between the peoples of the different parts of the country was forgotten in the excitement.

To all appearances life went on in the village of
Siba as usual, but this was due to the necessity for
actual living and eating. They must hunt continually for game, and pick berries, and gather seeds
for food whether their hearts and minds were in
a state of excited curiosity or not. The whole
village needed food.

So they had a rabbit hunt for which they burned
the dry grass. The Indians loved the excitement of
fire. The crackling and heat of the flames as they
raced over the brown grass, leaving blackened
shrubs and ashes behind, gave them a feeling of
exhilaration. For one thing, it drove all the little
animals of the fields to running hither and yon in
order to elude the heat. This was the object of
the fire, and arrows and throwing sticks were flying through the smoke at the frightened little
fugitives. Hares, rabbits, ground squirrels, rats,
field mice, and even snakes and grasshoppers, unable to flee the heat, added to their store of food
roasted for them by the fire.

The *Puplum* did not join in the rabbit hunt, nor
were they excited by the fire. They sat in the *Yoba*
and held council, for the news of the strangers in
their country, and all that could be told about them,
gave considerable anxiety to the *Puplum*. If these
beings were gods, as the people seemed to believe,
they did not come within any known conception of
the wise men. Their creeds and knowledge were
being put to the test, and the *Puplum* defied the

invasion of these new beings which, from the very first, they could not classify.

Pul Maat, who seemed even more concerned than any of the others, went into the chaparral one night to commune with Itaru, to get counsel through Itaru from Y-yo-ha-rivg-nain. He was gone several days, and when he returned he called the *Puplum* together. There was much activity after that within the sacred *Yobagnar*, from which the people were excluded.

Yamino-Kwiti had heard it said that Pul Maat would give the *Puplum* the counsel of Itaru. With his usual curiosity, he loitered about the *Yoba*, hoping to hear what this counsel might be. It was possible that he might be called in as a young *Púmal* for a part in some ceremony, so he lingered, but evidently this was only for the wise men; the children were not wanted—not even a *Púmal*. But all he could hear was the usual, muttered incantations in the sacred language, interminable in length; sudden blood-curdling outcries; dances with throbbing rhythm ending in grunts and roars like the sounds of the different animals. One would have thought he were outside a pen of animals if he did not know that only the men of the *Puplum* went into the single opening in the *Yoba*, and this was the usual procedure.

The boy's active curiosity could not endure the tedium of waiting till the long ceremony was ended, and he went off to hunt with the other boys.

He found the *Puplum* still carrying on their mysterious ceremony when he returned.

When it was finally ended, Siba-vik had Ya'ii-kat, the crier, call the people together. There was not room for all of them in the *Yoba*, so they sat in the great clearing in the center of the village, and Siba-vik talked to them.

There were strangers invading their country, he said, who were traveling slowly northward. They would soon be in this part of the country. From the reports brought to him by runners, these newcomers did not seem to be enemies. In fact, they came with presents and in the manner of friends.

The *Puplum* had had conference with Itaru, Siba-vik continued—Pul Maat lifted his head proudly—and Itaru had counseled them in this fashion: *the day of the Indian was ending, and the day of the white man was beginning.*

There was dead silence at this announcement, for it was impossible for the people to grasp the full meaning of this prophecy. How could the Indian day end? Had they not always been here in this pleasant valley? There was no knowledge among them of any other existence in any other place. Why should it not go on and on? They could not comprehend the idea of an ending! What did it mean?

It must have cost Pul Maat considerable moral effort to give this counsel from Itaru, for he opposed the coming of the strangers from the very first, fearful that the prediction was true.

All that was told to the people of Siba, however, of the white men—their strange animals and presents—aroused their curiosity and cupidity. These people did not pilfer their villages, kill their warriors, burn their houses, or capture their women and bear them away, and so they were not enemies. The prevailing good nature of the Indians made it natural for them to greet such harmless and curious people in friendly fashion.

Yamino-Kwiti and the other children spent much time talking about the strangers. They were always in evidence when runners came from the south to convey the latest tidings to Siba-vik. They squirmed under the arms of the elders into the crowd that gathered about the chief and the panting couriers. The older men were too absorbed in the purport of the messages to notice the children. Under ordinary circumstances they would have been denied the pleasure of squirming into the front row of listeners, but now the older people could talk of nothing but white men and gave little heed to the children.

One day, when Tamít was high in the sky, the seven giants who held up the earth on their shoulders got very restless and moved the earth until it trembled and shook. It frightened the people, and the members of the *Puplum* took it upon themselves to chastise the giants. They scolded and pleaded

and danced toward the four corners of the earth
with raised arms in an effort to pacify them and
felt reassured when the trembling ceased.

Late that afternoon the report came by courier
that the cavalcade of strangers was camping on
the riverbank to the south of them, near Hutuk.[8]

Yamino-Kwiti could stand it no longer. The
summer moon, when the grass was brown and
sear, was past its greatest fullness, but made good
light for traveling. He did not go to bed that night,
but, saying nothing to anyone, started out with
his throwing stick in his belt, his bow over his
shoulder, and his arrows in the quiver which hung
from his belt of fiber.

Long before dawn broke the swift-footed Yamino-Kwiti was hiding in the brush above the
camp of white men on the riverbank. The brush
was full of other Indians, old and young, men and
women, those who were still timid and not trustful
of these strangers. Indians from the village of
Hutuk across the river were mingling with the
white men in all friendliness, receiving gifts from
them and giving them seeds and meal in return.
They were talking to those strange Indians who
had come with the white men, clothed like them,
and who did not speak the language of Hutuk or
Siba. They managed, however, to make themselves
understood with the aid of many signs.

There were two strangers, different from the
others, who wore long ash-colored robes, wide-

brimmed hats, and a string of beads ending in a little cross, looped through the rope girdle around their waists. Their faces were smooth like the Indians'. The other white men wore beards upon their faces. Evidently they did not pluck their beards out as the Indians did, one hair at a time, with the little bivalve shells, as Yamino-Kwiti had seen the men do for one another.

Yamino-Kwiti watched with rapturous eyes. The whole camp was fast awakening. All about him he heard these people saying to one another, as they emerged from their sleeping quarters, *"Buenos dias, señor!"* He said it over and over to himself, "Boo-ayé-nos deé-ahs, sayn-yór," without understanding its cheery greeting.

He watched the Indians who, like the white men, wore garments to cover their brown bodies. They were working among the animals—and such animals! The strangers did not seem to be afraid of them, nor did the animals run away. They were even more docile than the Indian dogs, who barked from the outskirts at these newcomers. The creatures were unlike anything Yamino-Kwiti had ever seen before, unless it were the antelope or the deer. Some of them had short ears and some had long.

Yamino-Kwiti saw one of the men strike a long-eared creature on his rump, push him hard, and say, *"Una mala mula!"** and Yamino-Kwiti re-

* Una ma'-la moo'-lah—a bad mule.

peated the words to himself, "*Una mala mula, mala mula.*"

Then something happened that frightened him. One of the animals lifted his nose, bared his teeth, and, putting his long ears back against his head, gave such a convulsive, horrifying noise that the Indians from the village of Hutuk retreated in fright and dismay. The queer creature drew in gusty breaths and repeated the diabolical uproar again and again. Other creatures like him took up the challenge, and the air was full of a din unbelievable!

The frightened Indians fled into the brush from where they peered trembling and awed, waiting to see if the animals were as ferocious as they sounded, but the beasts did not follow them, and the strangers paid no attention to the noise and clamor. They went about their work of tending the creatures, slapping them on their rumps, leading them to the river to drink, and with many pushes and shouted directions let them eat the dry grass all about camp.

When the Indians, hiding timidly in the brush, saw that no one else was disturbed by the noise, they gradually stopped trembling and drew close again. In the reaction from an unnecessary fear they grew boisterous and mimicked the mules.

The bearded chief of the white men stood before his tent. He heard the laughter and apings of the Indians and laughed heartily. Those who gathered about him laughed also, looking toward the bushes where the hidden Indians had disclosed their whereabouts by their nervous burst of hilarity.

Others of the strangers came into sight from the shelters they had erected for sleeping. Yamino-Kwiti forgot where he was in his absorption of the scene before him and moved nearer. Indian boys are taught to move always with their senses alert. So many unexpected dangers lurk on every side that they must continually be seeing with their eyes and hearing with their ears. Now that Yamino-Kwiti had strange beings to observe, he saw details that, without doubt, escaped even the strangers themselves who saw them daily.

The Indians, watching from ambush, gradually overcame their timidity. One by one they emerged from their hiding to join the other natives from Hutuk and to receive their share of the presents which the gray-robed men gave them. Yamino-Kwiti mingled with them and went from one group to another. There was so much to see! With an ear trained for remembering, he listened to new words and phrases in a language as different from his own as the grunts of animals are different from the singing of birds and the rippling of waters.

He saw the preparation of strange food. He watched them eat with strange implements. One of the men, seeing him standing so near with a hungry expression in his eyes, offered him a *tortilla*.[48] He put his hand out eagerly and was about

Huge copper kettle used by the Spaniards
on their expedition.

to bite into it when one of the Hutuk Indians cried
out, "No, no! Do not eat the strangers' food!"

Yamino-Kwiti looked wonderingly at the speaker, then at the smiling face of the stranger. Deliberately and confidently he bit into the food. Finding it good, he consumed it in eager, Indian fashion.
There was a general laugh among the strangers.
They called him, *"Bueno muchacho,"* and repeating, with his mouth full, "Boo-ayé-no moo-chá-
cho," he wondered why they all laughed, for he
did not know that he was calling himself a "good
boy."

He watched them packing their belongings, wondering about the use of all these strange things.
Some of the Indians tried to take the things they
saw, but the strangers yelled at them and made
them give up everything they took except the presents which the gray-robed men gave them.

It was a most amazing sight to Yamino-Kwiti to see the animals stand patiently and allow great packs to be put on their backs and strapped tightly around their bodies. But when the animals brayed, he could not keep his fear of them in control and ran as fast as his feet could take him from that uncouth noise into the brush again. The white men only laughed at him and went on with their loading, so he stopped his trembling and came back to watch. Again they called him *"Bueno muchacho!"*

He heard an unfamiliar sound, one he had never heard before—the ringing of a bell! It seemed to intone through the air like an insistent warning and left him standing rooted to the spot, quivering. Then he saw that, as the sound continued, the strangers dropped whatever they were doing and followed it. So he, too, followed wonderingly with the others to where the whole assemblage of strangers knelt upon the earth. He could not understand what they were saying or doing, but he realized from their attitude of devotion that in some way they were worshiping Y-yo-ha-rivg-nain, but listen as he would he did not hear the name of the Great Giver of Life spoken by any of them. He did hear the words, however, *"Dios"* and *"Jesus"* and *"María,"* and uncomprehendingly pronounced them to himself: "Dee-os, hay-sus, ma-ree-ah."

He felt a strange ecstasy when they sang. The Spanish voices rang out in full, round tones, with an unbelievable sweetness. Their singing was not like his own people's, nor did they dance when they sang. Instead, they knelt upon the ground and raised their faces to the sky or bent them seriously over a string of beads. Yamino-Kwiti could not understand the gestures they made, nor the things that they said, but there was something restful and comforting about the voice of the man who stood in front of a strange graceful image, with his back to the assembly, and chanted in rich tones. Yamino-Kwiti liked it. For some reason he felt comforted and soothed and was sorry when it ended.

When the group broke up and scattered, going back to their loading, he watched the man in the beautiful vestments. He saw him take them off and stand again in his somber, gray robe. Yamino-Kwiti heard someone call this man by name, and he pronounced it over and over to himself: "Padre Crespi, Pa-dre Cres-pi."

Instantly the man turned to him and, smiling down at Yamino-Kwiti, put his hands on the boy's head and spoke to him. The Indian boy did not know that he had received a blessing from the very depths of the padre's heart. Yamino-Kwiti's training in the detested *Yoba*, when he had spent hours repeating the things Pul Maat had said to him, was now making it possible for him to remember the sounds he heard and to repeat them. This ability delighted Padre Crespi and his companion,

Padre Gomez, and the two men talked together about the boy.

Yamino-Kwiti, however, had other things to see, and he followed after the man with the blue coat, brass buttons, yellow vest, and leather leggings upon his legs. They called him *"Señor gobernador,"* and Yamino-Kwiti was fascinated with the unknown materials of which his uniform was made.

His eager attention was attracted to the man they called Señor Ortega, who put his foot into something that hung down from the saddle on a horse and swung himself up onto its back! Other men did the same thing, until there was a great number of them on the backs of the animals. This was a daring thing to do! Yamino-Kwiti could hardly subdue his fear of the horses as they pranced and cavorted and then galloped away in a great cloud of dust with the men upon their backs. He had never seen anything like that before!

It would have taken something stronger than curiosity or tribal allegiance to tear Yamino-Kwiti away from this group of white men now. He followed along with them as they broke camp and journeyed north, away from Hutuk, a small personification of wonder, learning a new language and new ways.

When the sun was high they stopped on a small hill near a pool of water not far from the Indian village of Sehat. All along the way the inhabitants

of Sehat had joined with those who followed from
Hutuk. There were Indians everywhere, watching
from the brush along the way with unmistakable
timidity. Some, having lost their fear, followed
along in the rear, not minding the dust kicked up
by the horses and mules of the rear guard. Other
Indians mingled with the forward group of "*soldados de cuero*," those who wore the leather coats
and shields. All of them watched greedily for
anything they could possess of the fascinating
things of the white men. They would have taken
their very garments, could they get their hands on
them, so great was their interest in colored fabrics
and metal implements.

The metal tools that fascinated the Indians.

Yamino-Kwiti had no eyes for his fellow Indians
—had he not seen them all his life? He was completely absorbed in the strangers, their clothes,
their utensils, their animals—all so different from
the things they used in Siba.

The people of Sehat were friendly with the white

men, and the chief of Sehat came to Don Gaspar
Portolá, the white chief, and offered them the hos-
pitality of the village if the white men would live
at Sehat. Yamino-Kwiti watched them make this
offer with a thrill of expectation and waited
breathlessly for the Indian interpreter, who came
with the white men, to translate the answer.

If they came, they would always be near! He
was, therefore, disappointed when the chief of the
white men made it known that they could not stay;
they were going farther north.

That night he stayed with the camp and curled
up on the ground near the fire when he could no
longer stay awake. Padre Crespi found him there
and covered him with a Mexican *serape*.[49] When
Yamino-Kwiti woke in the morning and found
the beautifully patterned blanket over him he felt
of it, rubbed it against his cheek, and marveled at
its texture and colors. Padre Crespi was standing
before him, smiling. *"Buenos dias, niño,"*[50] he said.
But when Yamino-Kwiti repeated after him,
*"Buenos dias, niño,"* Padre Crespi shook his head.
Pointing to himself he said, *"Padre! Buenos dias,
padre!"* Yamino-Kwiti repeated this greeting cor-
rectly with his boyish friendly smile, and the priest
was delighted. He patted Yamino-Kwiti on the
head.

Again Yamino-Kwiti watched the men load the
mules and saddle the horses. Repeating the words
he had learned the previous morning to the mule-

teers, *"Una mala mula!"* he made them laugh. He laughed with them, liking their friendliness.

He ate with the muleteers again and once more attended mass. With his retentive memory he learned so many words of the Spanish language that he attracted the attention of the bearded *"Señor gobernador,"* or Don Gaspar Portolá, and that quiet-eyed chief spoke to Yamino-Kwiti.

*"Como te llamas tu?"*[51] he asked, but Yamino-Kwiti could not answer him. By numerous signs Don Gaspar Portolá made Yamino-Kwiti understand that he wanted to know his name. Finally Yamino-Kwiti pointed to himself and said his own name.

"Yamino-Kwiti?" asked Portolá.

*"Sí, señor,"* answered Yamino-Kwiti, and Portolá exchanged glances with Padre Crespi.

"This child is unusually bright and quick in picking up our language," said Padre Crespi.

"He could be of great use to us as an interpreter," said Don Gaspar Portolá, "if we could have him with us long enough."

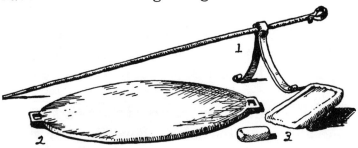

1. "Azador," or meat-toasting spit. 2. "Comal," or griddle for cooking "tortillas." 3. "Metatito," for grinding corn.

# 22

# Good-by, Siba!

THAT MORNING the party traveled across the hills beyond which lay Siba. Don Gaspar Portolá tried to keep Yamino-Kwiti with him as much as possible and to that end lifted him onto his own horse and let him ride behind him. Yamino-Kwiti was utterly speechless with fright but soon grew accustomed to the motion of the horse and lost some of his fear.

A long rattlesnake slowly undulated across the trail, and the horse stood on its hind legs and shied. Yamino-Kwiti almost fell off. His Indian training, however, caused him to act quickly. He slid from the horse and pulled his throwing stick from under his fiber belt where he had thrust it. He threw it so quickly and with such fierce precision that the

Rattlesnake.

snake lay writhing, with its head cut off completely by the sharp edge of the throwing stick.

"*Bravo!*" said Portolá. Yamino-Kwiti smiled up at him, but he was not willing to get on the horse again.

When they reached the river that flowed past Siba, the horses could not cross the gully, so they made camp on the bank of the stream while the men cut the willow trees for poles and constructed a bridge. The tools they used fascinated the Indians so greatly that the Spaniards had to watch them guardedly lest these necessary implements disappear. It was the first time the Indians had seen metal. They marveled at the hard shiny steel that was neither bone, wood, nor stone.

On the other side of the river Yamino-Kwiti saw his own people gathered, watching with curious intentness the construction of the bridge.

The women of his village came with baskets of chia seeds and acorn meal as favors to the strangers and received presents of ribbons and beads just as the other Indians along the line of march had done.

Some of the strangers went to hunt antelope, a herd of which could be seen in the distance beyond the burned patch where the Indians had hunted rabbits by fire. The villagers watched the hunters with inquisitiveness, but when they saw a soldier point his stick at an antelope, heard a loud bang, and saw the antelope drop in its tracks, they were astounded and frightened! It was a terrible noise. The frightened Indians scattered and disappeared into the brush and tall grass just as they had when the mules brayed.

The soldier who had shot the gun was proud of being a good shot and did not see the effects of his kill upon the Indians. They were in a state of consternation! There was some sort of magic about killing an animal with a loud noise from a stick. But could these beings be gods? Gods gave and sustained life—they did not take it! Thus they called the white men, *chichinabros*, "reasoning beings who were not gods."

When Yamino-Kwiti saw his mother's frightened face he ran to her.

"Ah, there you are, Little Runner!" she said. "Yamino-Kwiti, what was that terrible noise?"

"I do not know, Mother," he said. "All that they do is different from what we do!"

He went with his mother when she took her baskets of pinole to Padre Crespi. She was smiling and bashful when Don Gaspar Portolá, in blue and buff magnificence, let her know by signs that he favored her boy, Yamino-Kwiti.

That afternoon there was much to disturb the people of Siba as well as the white men, for the earth shook and trembled at repeated intervals. The Indians knew that the seven giants were again getting restless under their burden of holding up the world. Was the coming of the white men the cause? they asked themselves. Pul Maat was sure it was, and the prediction of Itaru filled him with gloom and unhappy forebodings in regard to the strangers.

The invaders called the place of encampment, "El Rio de los Temblores," "The River of the Earthquakes," and laughed at the efforts of Pul Maat to pacify the seven giants by shouting and waving his arms and jumping toward the four corners of the earth which they upheld.

That night when the Indians retired to their own village, Pul Maat was bitter in his predictions of the trouble that would come from the white men's invasion into the Indians' country. He recalled Itaru's forecast about the day of the Indian ending. Siba-vik felt, however, that there was more to be gained by friendliness than by any other attitude, and his wife smiled when she heard him, for she had her hands full of beautiful colored beads. Siba-vik himself had his thick black hair tied up with a gay red ribbon.

The next day's march took the Spaniards to a spot northwest of Siba. They went through such tall grass that the animals in the vanguard had to jump to get through it, in order to make a trail for those that followed. Not far from where they camped the ground was miry and the tules grew thick and tall. There were countless wild ducks and gray geese, and Yamino-Kwiti wondered at the white men's way of catching them. They shot them

"Bota para agua." Canvas canteen.

with the noisy sticks and, after picking up the ducks, threw away the beautiful feathers! Did they not know that feathers were for decorations in the *Yoba* and to be sewed into their ceremonial Tobet skirts and headdresses?

The Indians were intensely curious about these guns and tried in every way to examine them at close range, but the *soldados* guarded their arms carefully. The Indians could not manage to get near a single gun.

The greatest moment of Yamino-Kwiti's life came that morning. Through the interpreter, Portolá asked that the courier, Mamish-Ahikañ, his wife, and the chief of the village, Siba-vik, all come to him. Yamino-Kwiti flew like an arrow to do his bidding, and the two Spaniards, Don Gaspar and Padre Crespi, watched him as he sped over the ground as swift as a young deer.

"He will make an excellent courier," said Don Gaspar Portolá, thinking of the many messages he needed to send as he marched from point to point through this unknown country, determined to find the elusive bay of Monterey.

"He will also make a superior interpreter since he learns the language so quickly," answered Padre Crespi, who was thinking of the Indians he desired to reach that he might teach them the religion so dear to his heart, make Christians of them, and thus save their souls.

When the little group from Siba came together, Pul Maat came with them. He stood like a gloomy shadow of dire prediction behind Siba-vik and heard the Indian interpreter ask if the boy would be allowed to go with the white men on their journey to the north.

"They want you to be courier for the *chichinabros*, Yamino-Kwiti," whispered his mother to him. He stood speechless with delight and anticipation, showing all his white teeth in a broad smile.

"No, no!" shouted Pul Maat. "It shall not be!"

All turned to the old man in amazement, and the smile faded quickly from the face of Yamino-Kwiti, leaving him scowling at Pul Maat.

"Poor little boy!" said Padre Crespi to himself, as he saw the boy's disappointment.

Pul Maat did not give the interpreter an opportunity to translate to Don Gaspar Portolá. He talked so fast in his harsh voice that one could hardly follow him. The child should not go, he insisted; he was chosen for the *Puplum!* No one could deny the right of the *Puplum!*

Don Gaspar, sensing something of the difficulty, told them through the interpreter that they were all coming back in a short time. They were going north and returning. The boy could return to his people later.

Pul Maat was outdone. Mamish-Ahikañ, his wife, and Siba-vik all agreed that Yamino-Kwiti should go with the party when they broke camp the following morning. He was indeed a happy boy as he ran back to the village to spend his last night with his mother.

Yamino-Kwiti could hardly sleep that night, and long before dawn broke he was up, tucking his arrows into his quiver. With his bow and his throwing stick he was ready. He said good-by to his mother and Mamish-Ahikañ and crawled eagerly out of the wickiup into the gray dawn. He slipped quietly through the village and past each hut as silently as a shadow, faithful Wushi following close at his heels.

Fearful lest Pul Maat might try to stop him, he hurried on. Not far from the village he looked back. There, outside her father's hut, stood Kihut-Kiur, a wistful, lonely little figure; the only other one awake in all the village. He raised his hand above his head, stood still a moment until he saw her answer his gesture, then, as swift as a young deer, he bounded over the trail left by the white men. The tracks were plain, for the tall grass was trampled down and the hoofs of the horses had dug sharply into the black soil.

Flying along with winged feet and happy heart, he went toward the Spanish camp. He could already hear the mules braying, and the bell ringing that summoned the men to an early mass.

Yamino-Kwiti had said good-by to Siba! At last he was to be a courier and see the world! He was sure, now, that Y-yo-ha-rivg-nain had been pleased with his prayer offerings in the *Yobagnar.*

There stood Kihut-Kiur, a wistful, lonely little figure.

---

( 🐾 )

---

# Appendix and Notes

The Indians of this story were called "Gabrielino" Indians by the Spaniards because of the San Gabriel Mission which was built near the Indian village of Siba, or Sibanga. They were, however, of the Shoshonean stock, which included many local groups of varying dialects.

"The diversity of language is so great in California that almost every 12 or 20 leagues you find a distinct dialect so different that in no way does it resemble the others." (From J. P. Harrington's translation of Boscana's *Chichigchinich.*)

The names used are taken from "Shoshonean Dialects of California," U. of C. Publications, *American Archaeology & Ethnology,* Vol. IV, No. 3, University Press, Feb., 1907; and the *Handbook of the California Indian,* both by A. L. Kroeber, and are known words of this almost extinct language. The Spaniards described the language as very uncouth in sound, guttural and sputtering. The spelling is as close as it is possible to get with our own alphabet, for these Indians had no form of writing.

## Notes

1. *Siba-vik:* the termination "vik" signifies "chief" and is used after the name of the village itself, as *Asuksa-vik, Akura-vik,* etc.
2. Such words as "mother, father, brother," or parts of the body, were not used without the personal pronoun preceding it, as, for instance:
   *my* mother, *Ni-ok*
   *thy* mother, *Mo-ok*
   *his* or *her* mother, *A-ok*
   *my* father, *Ni-nack*
   *my* older brother, *Ni-apa*
   *my* younger brother, *Ni-apeitz,* etc.

3. *Yobagnar:* a place of worship which was circular and approximately in the center of the hamlet. The place was sacred but was consecrated each time it was used. Only the *Puplum*, or priesthood, were allowed in the *Yobagnar*. They sometimes took a whole day to consecrate the *Yobagnar* for any impending ceremony.

There was also an unconsecrated outer *Yoba*, used for rehearsing and training the children dedicated to this end.

The word *Yobagnar* (in the Luiseño dialect the word is *Vanquich*) has been translated at times as Church, or Temple, but neither of these translations gives the full meaning of the word. It was not a permanent construction and was frequently destroyed after use.

4. *Puplum:* the plural for *Pul*, or priest. An organization of wise men, rain makers, priests, etc., who held the control and government of the people in their hands. Even the chief was subject to its decisions.

5. *Mom-lah'-pish:* a bull-roarer, made of a flat stick with a double string passed through a hole in one end. When the string was twisted and swung around the head it made a drumming sound. It was used to call the people together.

6. The Gabrielino Indians had no word for "love." The nearest they came to it was *nonim uisminoc*, meaning, "I have regard, or affection."

7. *Mamish-Ahikañ: Mamish*, in the Luiseño dialect, means an unencumbered one, and was applied to the couriers who ran without any encumbrance whatever. The couriers were trained for the work when young and were used until worn out. *Ahikañ* signified "wind," the name given the courier because he was as fleet as the wind.

8. Indian Villages and Settlements:

Ahachmai, San Juan Capistrano, on San Juan Creek, in Juaneño territory.
Akura, now known as La Presa. In Gabrielino territory.
Asuksa, an Indian village near Asuza, in Gabrielino territory.
Hutuk, an Indian village north of Santa Ana, on the Santa Ana River, Gabrielino territory.

Kukomo, or Cucumonga, an Indian village near Cucumonga Peak, northeast of Pomona.

Mukupiabet, an Indian village in Cajon Canyon north of San Bernardino in Serrano territory.

Nipawai, near the San Diego Mission, in Diegueño territory. The Diegueños were enemies of the Gabrielinos.

Pala, an Indian settlement on the San Luis Rey River, near Pala Mission, Luiseño territory. A Luiseño word meaning "water."

Pieakhehe, or Paiakche, now known as Lake Elsinore, in Luiseño territory.

Shua, one of the largest of the Indian villages, on the present site of Long Beach.

Sisitkano, now known as Pear Orchard.

Tahachapi, Indian settlement near Tehachapi Pass.

Toibi, near Pomona, Gabrielino territory.

Wachbit, a hamlet near San Bernardino, on the Santa Ana River, in Serrano territory.

Wenot, a hamlet near Rancho La Brea.

Wiawio, on the shore near Oceanside, west of San Luis Rey Mission.

Yan, or Yangna, an Indian village near the old section of Los Angeles.

The termination "ngna" seemed to mean "the place of" when attached to the name of a village or hamlet. Hence, Siba became Sibanga, Yan became Yanga, Kukomo, Kukamonga. In the territory east of San Gabriel, the termination "bit" or "bet" seemed to mean the same as the Gabrielino "ngna, nga," or "gna."

9. Song fight: a typical Indian institution, formed upon their hate of their enemies. See Chapter 13.

10. The name "Tomear" and "Manisar" were terms used for the eldest son and daughter, respectively, of the chief, regardless of any other appellation they may have earned.

11. Kwawar: the name of their deity which was seldom spoken and never aloud. *Y-yo-ha-rivg-nain* was the spoken word which means "The Giver of Life." There were three phases of their Deity: *Saor,* the latent phase; *Tobet,* the active phase (from which they derived their ceremonial dance with the Tobet feathered skirt) ; and *Kwawar,* or that which follows active expression—the Deity who, after ascending to heaven, dwells among the stars and watches from above.

12. Their year began at the winter solstice, when "Tamít

came out of his house." The months did not corre-
spond to our own, since they were reckoned by the
moon and the seasonal conditions about them.

> January, *Aapcomil*—The Month of Cold, and Hunting.
> February, *Peret*—The Month of Rain, or Little-Tree-Sprout-
> ing Month.
> March, *Yarmar*—The Big-Tree-Sprouting Month.
> April, *Alasoguil*—The Green Grass Month, or The Rise of
> Waters.
> May, *Tocoboaich*—The Month of Roots.
> June, *Sintecar*—When the Young Eagles Fly.
> July—part of *Sintecar* and part of *Cucuat*.
> August, *Cucuat*—The Brown and Sear Month.
> September, *Lalavaich*—The Gray Goose Month, or that of
> Wild Fruits.
> October, *Aguitscomel*—The Wind-Whistling Month.
> November, *Aaguit*—The Big Wind-Whistling Month, or Nuts
> and Acorns.
> December, *Aapcomil*—The Month of Cold, and Hunting.

13. False deer heads were used by the men in hunting
deer. They would draw the folds of the neck over
their shoulders and stalk among the chaparral, occasionally allowing the browsing deer to see the false
head above the tops of the brush, thus stealing up
close to the unsuspecting animals.

14. Pimu: the island of Santa Catalina. The people were
of the same stock and spoke the same dialect as those
of Siba.

15. Throwing stick: called *makana* (probably by the
Spaniards). It was similar to the boomerang of the
Australians, but it is not known that they were able
to throw it so that it returned to them. They were,
however, very skillful with it.

16. Now called the San Gabriel River.

17. El Puente Hills.

18. *Nio-mare:* an untranslatable expression used much as
we would say, "Bless me!"

19. *Ponko:* a length of money beads that measured about
thirty inches. Four *ponko* equaled a *sayako*.

20. *Yamu uimi:* "I am going." *Mea,* "Go!" This was the
customary form of farewell, as distinctly Indian as
*Adios* is Spanish, and *Aloha-oe* is Hawaiian.

21. Taquich: the demon of the ball lightning who lived in the canyon of San Jacinto Mountain. Tauwaro: the god of thunder.

22. The canoe builders were the Coastal Indians of Santa Barbara and Ventura. They made the canoes of planks and literally sewed them together with thongs, calking with asphaltum.

23. Tar Pits: Rancho La Brea, in Los Angeles, which recently yielded the entire skeletons of prehistoric animals, now on exhibit at the Los Angeles Museum. The Indians of the vicinity used the tar for water-proofing their baskets, since they made no pottery.

24. Steatitic pots: made by the people of Pimu, or Santa Catalina Island, and traded with the shore Indians for other commodities. Steatite, or soapstone, was found only in this locality, and very beautiful pots were made of it.

25. The California condor is rapidly becoming extinct. It is a direct descendant of the huge vulture trapped in the quaternary asphalt of Rancho La Brea in the Pleistocene period. It was an immense bird, with a wingspread of over ten feet, sometimes fourteen or fifteen feet.

26. The ceremony in commemoration of the dead was held about a year after the funeral, and for this purpose they kept a few of the dead person's trinkets and a lock of the hair.

27. *Alala:* an expression used much as we would say, "Well, well!" or "Goodness me!"

28. *Pukú, wehé, páhe:* one, two, three.
*Mahar*, five, and *wehés mahar*, ten, or two times five.

29. *Sanot:* the Indian term for asphaltum.

30. *Amole* root: soap root, or *chlorogalum pomeridianum*, a plant of the lily family, peculiar to California.

31. Agave fiber: fiber taken from the leaves of the agave plant, a member of the cactus family.

32. Apaches: Indians of the desert area and east of the San Bernardino Mountains, much to be dreaded.

33. *O-a nahacua:* literally, "you hear." The criers went about the hamlet calling to the people to listen to the tale of crime of the one about to be tried by council, thus working up a feeling against him.

34. Mourning mask: made of the ashes from the funeral pyre and mixed with water. This mixture was smeared over the face of the mourner and left there until it wore off—the period of mourning then being over.

35. *Shu-shyot:* the stars which they believed to be dead chiefs, or the souls of those who escaped death.

36. Mayaintalap: the Big-Bow people, from north of Tehachapi.

37. The Indian girls were tattooed in their infancy as a rule, although this practice was not always carried out until about their tenth year. The marks were drawn vertically from eyebrows down across the chin and over their arms and breasts. The skin was pricked with a cactus thorn and rubbed with agave charcoal which left a blue stain or scar.

38. Leaching: the acorn is too bitter to eat in its natural state, even for the Indian, and an elaborate preparation was required to make it palatable. After cracking the acorns the kernels were ground to a meal in stone mortars with stone pestles. After the grinding the meal was placed in a finely woven basket and placed in a shallow place in the sand. Water was then poured over it, which carried the bitter tannin contained in the acorn into the sand. The meal was then either used to make cakes or dried for future use.

39. *Ycuaro:* "Here," or "Here I am."

40. *Churchurki:* "Sports and games were few. The principal one was *Churchurki*, or Peon, as it is called by the Spaniards. It consists of guessing in which hand a small piece of stick was held concealed by another. Four persons on a side composed a set, who sat opposite each other. They had their singers, who were paid so much a game, and an umpire who kept count, held the stakes, settled disputes, and prevented cheat-

ing. He was paid so much a night, and had to provide the firewood. He was provided with fifteen counters, which were of reed and eight or ten inches long. The guessers never spoke, but giving the palm of the left hand a sharp slap with the right pointed with the finger to the side they guessed contained the peon. Those who guessed right won the peon, and the others took a counter, each, and so on, until they possessed all the counters, or lost all the peons, when the opposite side took the counter part.

"The peon was white, of an inch or two in length; but they had also a black one, which, to prevent fraud, they had to remove to the other hand, on changing, so as always to retain one in each hand, to show when called upon. This was their favorite game, and they at times bet their all on it ... bystanders take as much interest and wager as heavily as those principally concerned." Reid, Hugo, *Indians of Los Angeles County*.

41. Sweat house: one or more of these were always in evidence in each village. They were used chiefly for curing sickness or purification of the body. They were dug out of the earth and were about as airtight as they could be made, with only one opening, and that a small one. They were usually heated by hot stones.

42. Sacred language: the *Puplum* used a "court language" not entirely understood by the layman.

43. *Mututci:* fleas. These were so thick in the Indian habitations that the Spaniards called one of their camp sites, Las Pulgas, the Spanish term for fleas.

44. *Wehés-mahar:* see note 28.

45. Sand painting: a ground painting, made of colored sands. Usually destroyed after serving a ceremonial purpose.

46. *Cuwot:* a mysterious bird, never seen, nor proved, but whose cry was thought to be *"Cu, cu,"* in the night. Tales were told of its carrying people away.

47. *Zizu:* supposed to be a demon who could track his victim by scent as a dog does.

48. *Tortilla:* a flat Mexican cake made of corn meal.

49. *Serape:* a Mexican blanket.

50. *Buenos dias, niño:* Spanish for "Good day, little boy." *Muchacho* also means "boy," but *niño* is used for "little boy" or "little child," and Padre Crespí so used it. He regarded the Indians as "his children," and the boy, Yamino-Kwiti, was to him a little child, so he called him *"niño,"* while the muleteers called him *"muchacho."*

51. *Como te llamas tu?* The Spanish way of asking, "What is your name?" Literally, "What do you call yourself?"

PUBLISHER'S NOTE (1983 EDITION): Two errors of natural history should be noted. Wild honey and watercress, both mentioned in this book, were introduced into California only after the coming of whites.

# Pronounciation of Indian Words Used in Yamino-Kwiti

Ahikañ—Ah-hee-kahng

Akura—Ah-koo-rah

Amole (Spanish)—Ah-mo-lay

A-nub-su-voi-rot—Ah-nub-soo-voey-rot

Anusetaxai—Ah-noo-sey-tah-high

Ashawut—Ah-sha-wut

Asuksa—Ah-sook-za

Cabatcho—Cah-baht-cho

Chamuca—Chah-moo-kah

Chichinabros—Chee-chee-nah-bros

Chukít—Choo-keet'

Churchurki—Chur-chur-kee

Coyote (Spanish)—Ko-yo'-tay

Crúmi—Kroo'-mee

Cuwot—Shoo-wot

Fúmi—Foo'-mee

Hararicuar—Ha-rah-ree-koo-ar

Hunar—Hoo-nar

Hutuk—Hoo-tuk

Icauvut—E-kaw-vut

Itaru—E-tar-oo

Kicha-Shungal—Kee-cha-Shoon-gal

Kihut-Kiur—Kee-hoot-Kee-oor

Kitúmi—Kee-too'-mee

Koti-Cuit—Ko-tee-Koo-eet

Kukomo—Koo'-ko-mo

Kwawar—Qua-war

Mamish-Ahikañ—Mah-meesh-Ah-he-kang

Manisar—Mahn-ee-sar

Mayaintalap—Mah-yine-tah-lap

Mea—May-ah

Moar—Mo-are

Momati—Mo-mah'-tee

Mom-lah-pish—Mom-lah'-peesh

Muhut—Moo-hut

Muka-Ayoin—Moo-kah-Ah-yoen

Mukupiabet—Moo-koo-pe-ah-bet

Mututci—Moo-toot-see

Nanah—Nah-nah

Ni-apa—Nee-ah-pah

Nipawai—Nee-pah-wy

Nio-mare—Nee-o-mah-ray

O-a nahacua—O-ah nah-ha-quah

Páhe—Pah'-hay

Pala—Pah-lah

Panes—Pah-nays
Páymi—Pahee-me
Pieakhehe—Pee-ay-ahk-hey-hey
Pimu—Pee-moo
Ponko—Pon-ko
Pukú—Poo-koo′
Puku-Kakar—Poo-koo′-Kah-kar
Pul Eraxbu—Pool Er-ash-boo
Pul Maat—Pool Mah-ot
Pul Sacasca-Tatma—Pool Sah-kahs-ka-Taht-ma
Pumal—Poo-mahl
Puplum—Poop-loom
Puy-Puy—Poo-ee-Poo-ee

Rómi—Roh′-mee

Saor—Sah-ore
Sayako—Sah-yah-ko
Sehat—Say-hot
Siba-vik—See-ba-veek
Sierra Madre (Spanish)—See-ay′-rah Mah′-dray
Sintecar—Sin-tay-kar
Sisitkano—See-seet-kah-no
Shukat—Shoo-kaht
Shu-shyot—Shoo-shyot
Soldados de cuero (Spanish)—Sol-dah′-dos dey koo-er′-o

Tahachapi—Tah-ha′-cha-pe
Tamít—Tah-meet′
Taquich—Tah-queech

Tauwaro—Tow-wah-ro
Tcoar—Cho-are
Tobet—Toh-bet
Tocoboaich—Toe-ko-bo-iche
Toibi—Toy-bee
Toloache—Toh-low-ah′-chay
Tomear—Toh′-may-are
Tucupar—Too-koo-par
Tukut—Too-kut

Wachbit—Wahch-bit
Wehé—Wey-hay
Wehés-mahar—Wey-hays-mah-har
Wenot—Way-not
Wikuam—Wee-koo-ahm
Wupu-Yatcho—Woo-poo-Yaht-cho
Wushi—Woo-she

Xai—Shy

Ya'iikat—Yah-ee-ee-kat
Yamino-Kwiti—Yah-mee′-no-Quee′-tee
Yamu-uimi—Yah-moo-oo-eem-ee
Yangna—Yahng-nah
Yayare—Yah-yah-ray
Ycuaro—E-koo-ar-o
Yobagnar—Yo-bagn-nar
Y-yo-ha-rivg-nain—E-yo-ha-riv-ngine

Zizu—Zee-zoo

# Bibliography

To make this clearer, the references below are the references contained in Zahrah Preble Hodge's notebook —a very scholarly work.

Arthur Woodward of Los Angeles Museum.

Reid, Hugo, *The Indians of Los Angeles County*.

Wagner, Henry, *Spanish Voyages to the Northwest Coast*.

Harrington, John P., *Chichigchinich*, Translation of Father Boscana's.

Kroeber, Alfred L., *Handbook of the California Indian*.

Curtis, Edward S., *The North American Indian*, Vol. XV.

Saunders, Chas. Francis, *With the Flowers and Trees in California*.

Bolton, Herbert Eugene, *Anza*, Vol. I.

U. of C. Publications, *American Archaelogy & Ethnology*, Vol. XX.

FURTHER REFERENCES:

Amsden, Charles, "Homo Californianus," *Touring Topics*, Nov., 1929.

Bolton, Herbert E., *Diary of Pedro Fages, U. of C. Academy Pacific Coast History Publications*, Vol. II, No. 3, pp. 141-59, 1911.

Cleland, *Pathfinders*.

Engelhardt, Fr. Zephyrin, *The Missions and Missionaries of California*.

Hemert-Engert, Adolph Van, and Teggart, Frederick J., eds., *The Narrative of the Portolá Expedition of 1769-70* by Miguel Costansó. *U. of C. Academy Pacific Coast History Publications*, Vol. I, No. 4, pp. 91, 159. 1910.

Hittell, Theodore H., *History of California*, Vol. I.

Bancroft, H. H., *History of California*.

Hess, Chester Newton, "Moccasin Joe," *Touring Topics*, May, 1930. "Outlaw Troubadour," *Touring Topics*, Nov., 1929. "King Condor," *Touring Topics*, Aug., 1930.

Holder, Charles Frederick, *Adventures of Torqua*.

Holmes, Wm. Henry, *Anthropoligical Studies in California*. Report of National Museum, 1900.

Mills, Enos A., *The Grizzly*. Houghton Mifflin Co.

*Pacific Coast History Publications, Academy of*—*Portolá's Journey through Los Angeles County*. Vol. I, No. 3, University of California, 1910.

Parsons, *The Wild Flowers of California*.

Rice, Bertha, *California Wild Flowers*.

Reusch, H. E. and E. G., *Historic Spots in California*.

Smith, Donald Eugene, account of *Portolá's Diary*.